Brill Walks

in the Peak and Dales

Book Two

Circular walks in and around
Matlock
Bakewell
Birchover
Youlgrave

Photographs: Bob Brill
Tales: Freda Bowman
Maps: Roger Penney

Freda Bowman   1   Bob Brill

Stiles come
in all styles

Introduction

The success of our first book, 'Brill Walks in the Peak', has encouraged us to produce this second one. It has been wonderful to learn that so many people have been introduced to walking, and taken pleasure in using our book. It is also encouraging to know that it has been equally appreciated by more seasoned walkers.

Like the first book, this one consists of twelve thoroughly researched walks. Again, the walks are all based around fairly close, but distinct areas of the Peak and Dales. This time the four areas are Matlock, Bakewell, Birchover and Youlgrave. Each walk has much to offer in terms of beauty, variety and points of interest, and we feel confident that, once again, the first one you attempt will encourage you to walk the others.

We have taken immense care to make the route instructions clear and totally confusion free, so that although simple maps are provided, these are intended only as general indicators of the point you have reached on the route. Nor is it assumed that you will carry an Ordnance Survey map, although starting point grid references are given. The walks have all been carefully checked by friends and family in order to ensure there are no areas of uncertainty.

However, it is important to remember that the countryside is a living environment, so changes can occur. A stile, for example, may be replaced with a gate, etc. We have tried to minimise the possible effects of changes by the style of instructions we use and the choice of waymarkers to guide you.

Particular points of interest are highlighted on each walk and we hope these will add to your enjoyment. It's the next best thing to having a local guide with you!

These circular walks vary in length and in terrain and the general summary before each one will help you to make your choice. In the beautiful Derbyshire countryside it is very difficult to avoid a few hills, and we are assuming our walkers are of normal health and fitness. It's worth a mention that our walks have been enjoyed by people of all ages.

Because many surfaces are uneven and certain areas can sometimes be muddy, lightweight walking boots are recommended for all our walks.

But the walks are not all we hope you will get from this book. For each of the four areas, in which the walks are located, there is a short narrative. Each is set in an interesting time of that place's history. The general details of the historical settings are researched and accurate. Four very different people, with contrasting lives, tell their own stories. We hope you will take even greater pleasure in walking each area after reading these tales.

We have thoroughly enjoyed both walking and writing our second book and our great wish is that you enjoy it too!

Contents

The Matlock Walks

Riber Castle

Bonsall Village Cross

The Spa Lady's Tale

It was certainly not my decision that we should go there - it was Humphrey's. It seems he had the right to make such decisions, in his role of man of the house and sole provider. I had never before visited any part of Derbyshire, had barely heard of Matlock. As for staying in a building owned and run by a John Smedley, I had my fears. The name suggested tradesman or mill worker (in this, of course, I was not wholly mistaken). But as Humphrey put forward his reasons for the visit, I was considerate enough to conceal the strength of my doubts. For some years, Humphrey had suffered badly from rheumatism, and occasionally from gout. "Too much rich food," our doctor had muttered, "and too little exercise." Not to mention, of course, a family disposition. His parents - God rest them - had scarcely been able to rise out of their chairs by the age of sixty.

Someone at the bank must have passed on to Humphrey that odd manual which he brought home. 'Practical Hydropathy' by 'John Smedley of Lea Mills', the heavy tome announced, 'including Plans of Baths' and 'Remarks on Diet and Habits of Life'. Well, my habits of life were certainly not up for scrutiny by any John Smedley, mill owner of Derbyshire. But Humphrey's apparently were, not that he had ever heeded a word of advice from me or from our doctor.

He proceeded to devour this ill-written manual and to discuss its contents with the obsessive zeal of a religious convert. Hydropathy, Humphrey now believed, was the answer to all his bodily ailments. This, of course, meant weird water treatments of various kinds. Water was the cure, the salvation, it would work the miracles that medicine could not. I myself felt the notion to be completely absurd - I am not a doctor's daughter for nothing, and I am not prone to being taken in by myth, magic or unscientific nonsense. Nor was Humphrey, I had previously supposed. He was hardly a man of romantic leanings, of that I had ample evidence. Indeed, he had always shown a tedious degree of a reasoned judgement. But in this matter he was won over, as so many others were, showing a pathetic trust in the curative power of water.

A decision was made before he had even reached the book's halfway point. We were to reserve a room at the great Smedley's Hydro in Matlock, Derbyshire. We would remain there for three weeks and he, at least, would submit himself willingly to whatever water treatments Mr. Smedley considered appropriate. We would enjoy the simplicity and plainness of the food set before us, listen carefully to all advice given, attend a daily religious service and be in bed each night by ten o'clock at the latest. For these privileges, we would happily pay Mr. Smedley two guineas each per week.

Just a month or so later, therefore, in the early June of 1864, I accompanied him north, and not with good grace. For myself, I should have much preferred to go to the city of Bath, where at least good shopping and social entertainment would be on offer, along with the nonsense of the waters. Matlock, I suspected, would offer little of either. But Humphrey was fixed upon a retreat to this simple, northern village - I doubted it could be given a label of 'town'.

My mood was not lifted on our eventual arrival at Matlock Bridge Station, in a heavy downpour of rain. At least the train journey had passed without problems. "If the worst comes to the worst," the thought struck me, "I can at least get myself back to London with reasonable ease." (A fake letter, concerning the illness of a relative, could be arranged if necessary). A small carriage met us - a carriage from Smedley's met every train apparently. The elderly driver briefly introduced himself as Fred, and after heaving our considerable luggage aboard, proceeded to drive us up a frighteningly steep hill. I felt sorry for the two horses pulling our weight, their metal shoes sliding at times on the wet and uneven surface.

As we rose, 'Smedley's' loomed before us. A vast and dark stone building, far more imposing than I had imagined, but severe and brooding in appearance. If not an eyesore, then certainly not a thing of beauty. Despite my foreboding, I was aware of a certain curiosity. Whatever went on it in that place, it was performed on a grand scale. As we drew up to the entrance, at the rear of the building, Humphrey put some question to our driver, but the reply was unclear - heavily disguised in a strong Derbyshire brogue. In London, such speech would have aroused a curious amusement.

We were politely received in the huge entrance hall, and as Humphrey signed the arrival book, I noted the building's impressive, though plain, interior. Our bedroom turned out to be very spacious also, grand even, though completely without frills or special comforts. I have to admit that the view from its high windows, as the rain now cleared and the sky began to brighten, was impressive. Not that I am overly enamoured of views - they hardly provide merry entertainment. Before leaving us to ourselves (what a dreary thought that was) the steward, who had shown us to our room, felt obliged to issue a reminder concerning the House Rules. "No alcohol is allowed in any part of the building," he unsmilingly announced, without so much as a hint of apology. We were aware of this already, of course. Humphrey had accepted it as a necessary part of his cure. For myself, I had concealed a bottle of brandy inside my luggage and felt sure that a large tot would be needed that very night. "No sweet items should be consumed between meals," the fellow droned on. "Our meals are very wholesome and are always followed by stewed fruit or a simple pudding." Well, even Matlock boasted a few shops, I had noted. Humphrey could forego whatever he wished.

I have to say that first evening meal came as something of a relief. The food was indeed plentiful enough, though very plain - Mr. Smedley, I was told, did not approve of either sauces or rich flavours. There were far more guests present in the huge dining room than I had foreseen - around a hundred, and it quickly became clear that people of good background from all over the country were present, and indeed from beyond. Tables were arranged in long rows and I found myself seated next to a very pleasing looking German gentleman, whose English was almost impeccable. Humphrey was seated at the other side of the table, but not quite opposite, so I felt perfectly justified in leaving him to his own conversational devices, which sadly were few.

Herr Schmidt, it transpired, was travelling on business throughout the North of England, and had decided that a week or so in the famous Matlock Hydro would be a pleasant interlude in an otherwise busy schedule. It soon transpired that he was staying there alone, though his domestic situation was not entirely clear. I immediately suspected he was a gentleman with an eye for the ladies. Nothing wrong with that, of course, provided it is accompanied by some charm, as indeed it was. Humphrey, for many years, had shown neither the eye nor the charm.

I was much amused to learn that Herr Schmidt had already fallen foul of the Smedley House Rules, by entering a lady's bedroom to return a silk scarf left on the sun seats outside. The lady in question, a widow, had been most appreciative, but this heinous deed had been spotted and reported by some beady eyed steward. My German companion had been asked to pay a fine of half a guinea and been formally reprimanded. We were both highly amused by this, and I silently resolved that should I ever wish to see him in private, I would take greater care than had the luckless widow.

The dining occasion having been surprisingly pleasant, I felt a keen sense of disappointment when a tinkling hand bell drew the tables to silence. Then Mr. John Smedley himself was announced, and an exceedingly ordinary looking man, probably in his sixties, rose from the other table and walked to the front, an open bible in his hand. He proceeded to read a - mercifully quite short - piece of scripture. This was not the end of it, however. No sooner had the bible closed and I had turned once again towards the fascinating Herr Schmidt, than Mr. Smedley addressed us further. "I now wish to say a few words to the gentlemen present", he stated, "concerning the abominable practice of smoking." I hoped Humphrey would listen - his clothes always reeked of tobacco smoke and snuff.

Mr. Smedley spoke with fervour and absolutely without trace of humour. As he returned to his place, I noted the woman I presumed to be his wife. Considerably younger than him, was my impression. A pleasant enough face, but no beauty. She had an air of piety around her - not at all the sort of woman, I imagined, that Herr Schmidt would be pleased to find himself seated next to. No doubt she and Mr. Smedley were admirably suited. Probably very rich also, I now suspected, despite their gospel of plainness and simplicity.

Following this, many people wandered into the large and fairly comfortable sitting room. Card playing was strictly forbidden. We were expected to rest, not even to talk, perhaps to listen to some hymns from the piano. Again Herr Schmidt was a surprise. "Would you care to hear a little music?" he asked me, the slight accent quite disarming. "If you like, I will play for you." I did indeed like, and positioned myself smilingly at the end of a rather hard sofa, close to the piano. Humphrey, somewhat conveniently, had approached Mr. and Mrs. Smedley after the meal, and was engaged in earnest discourse with them. This was briefly interrupted a few minutes later, midway through the delightful playing of a Chopin waltz.

"Herr Schmidt," Mrs. Smedley almost whispered to my friend, "we normally permit only sacred music to be played." "Madam," was his instant reply, "to me all music is sacred." She withdrew with a slight blush. All my favourable impressions of the pianist were confirmed.

Whatever the nature of Humphrey's discussion with the Smedleys, it inspired him with even greater zeal for his forthcoming treatments. These would begin promptly at six-thirty in the morning, when he would take himself along the corridor to bathroom number seven. His appointed bath man would then administer an extremely cold - just short of freezing -

dousing of water all over the body, while Humphrey sat in a shallow tub of equally cold water. This would be followed by his being wrapped from head to toe in wet sheets, soaked in slightly warmer water. The whole process would take well over an hour, a time that I fully intended to spend asleep. Later in the day, two further treatments would be undertaken, probably involving the leg bath. Hot mustard poultices would be applied to his knee and ankle joints, these being his most severe problem areas.

During the middle part of the day, Humphrey informed me, he would spend time in the library or take a few gentle strolls with me around the grounds. Unless, of course, I decided to take a carriage with other guests into Matlock Bath and the surrounding countryside. This was unhesitatingly my preference.

Of course, there was a minor battle to be fought. The devout Mrs. Smedley, it seemed, had charge of all women's treatments, and apparently she was expecting to have a consultation with me, to discuss any physical problems I might have. "Especially women's problems," poor, embarrassed Humphrey informed me. He was plainly anxious that I should avail myself of the kind offer. Naturally, I had no intention of doing so. The only woman's problem from which I suffered was a lack of entertaining male company, and this lack seemed likely to be unexpectedly relieved during our stay here.

Like Humphrey, Herr Schmidt availed himself of the water treatments - though only in the early morning, and involving nothing so drastic as mustard. He found the experience bracing, so he told me, though he shared my view that it was unlikely to cure any real ill. Indeed, he had no ills! He seemed to me to be in excellent health, possibly rather younger than myself, though I never inquired. It would have been irksome to have to lie. He regretted, he told me, that treatments were administered only by bath attendants of the same sex. On the continent, it was inferred, things could be very different. It was not a suggestion he thought worthwhile putting to Mr. and Mrs. Smedley.

A coach and horses took us out most afternoons, though sadly always in the company of others. Most people spoke of Mr. Smedley with great respect. A deeply religious man, I was informed, who himself had been won over to hydropathy after using it to recover from a serious breakdown. This breakdown, both mental and physical, had occurred some years ago, while the Smedleys were actually abroad on their honeymoon. ("What failures or disappointments had perhaps befallen them?" Herr Schmidt quietly mused). From the time of his cure, John Smedley had committed his life to hydropathy, and his devoted wife, Caroline, along with him. Early experiments were conducted on the workers in his textile mill and the vast Smedley building was the result of their apparent success. Many more centres had been set up by others, with his encouragement. Matlock Bank, as that hillside is known, was a veritable land of hydros, of which his own was the largest.

The departure of Herr Schmidt a few days before our own (he had already extended his stay by more than a week), was deeply depressing, almost as much as Henry's enthusiasm with his new sense of well-being. I did have to admit that he looked better, though I felt convinced that forgoing drink, tobacco and large quantities of meat provided a much likelier explanation than wet sheets. Sadly, there is no simple cure for the personality.

My spirit of curiosity was lifted slightly by a surprise invitation to dine at the home of
Mr. and Mrs. Smedley. Humphrey must indeed have impressed as a model patient. Home,
as I already knew, was that Gothic pile, perched high above Matlock. None other than
Riber Castle, on Riber Hill, designed and built by John Smedley for himself and his wife,
just a couple of years previously. The rumoured cost was sixty thousand pounds.

So it was that we were conveyed that evening, by John Smedley's personal carriage,
up the cruelly steep lanes leading finally to their castle's entrance. The main door was
positioned at the back of the building, to avoid bitter winds entering the house from across
the Derwent Valley. The place was cavernous, chilly even on that pleasant evening of late
June, though comfortably furnished and lit up, as the evening drew on, by gas lamps.
These, we were told, were powered from a small gasworks, built nearby by Mr. Smedley,
for that very purpose. I wondered what possessed the two of them to choose to live in such
a place, bereft even of the noise and company of children. Lack of children, of course, was
something we all shared.

The table was generous, and the evening passed affably enough. I was again struck by the
strength of John Smedley's convictions and by his desire to sway others towards them. This
was not a man to allow a moment of self-doubt to alter his course, and his sense of being
right was matched only by his utter contempt of the medical profession. His wife
noddingly agreed with every word he uttered. His purpose was clearly her purpose also,
and both seemed to work quite tirelessly. I have to admit I found them unappealing -
intense and humourless - though part of me envied Caroline her strong drive and purpose.
Women of wealth, at that time, had little sense of purpose in their lives, and much
boredom. I myself was an example.

Of course, this was all a very long time ago, more than thirty years in fact. Mr. Smedley
died some twenty years ago, at the age of seventy-one, and I cannot imagine so unique a
character in charge of a business now. Caroline died only two years ago. Surprisingly, we
remained in touch during the eighteen years of her widowhood, a state I too was to enjoy
for much of that time. During those eighteen years, she remained alone - unbelievably -
in the vast and eerie Riber Castle, continuing her work as ardently as before. She was an
admirable woman, but I have to admit to a great relief that she never accepted my
occasional invitations to travel with me to the continent.

The great Hydro continues, now under different management, and more relaxed, more
luxurious. A far cry from the strict and spartan regime to which we submitted. In the
future, it will no doubt be put to some other use. I cannot imagine that the silly myth of
hydropathy will survive forever. I'm quite convinced it cured no one, and brought a much
quicker end to quite a few!

As for Riber Castle, heaven knows what its future will be. Since Caroline's death, it has
become a small boarding school for boys, but I cannot see that lasting long. Who would
choose to send their son to such a desolate place? Though that's hardly a concern for me.

Should you ever find yourself in Matlock, you will hardly fail to notice its castle, looming
over the place like a ghostly sentinel. It dominates that town as surely as its creator,
Mr. John Smedley, once did.

Walk 1

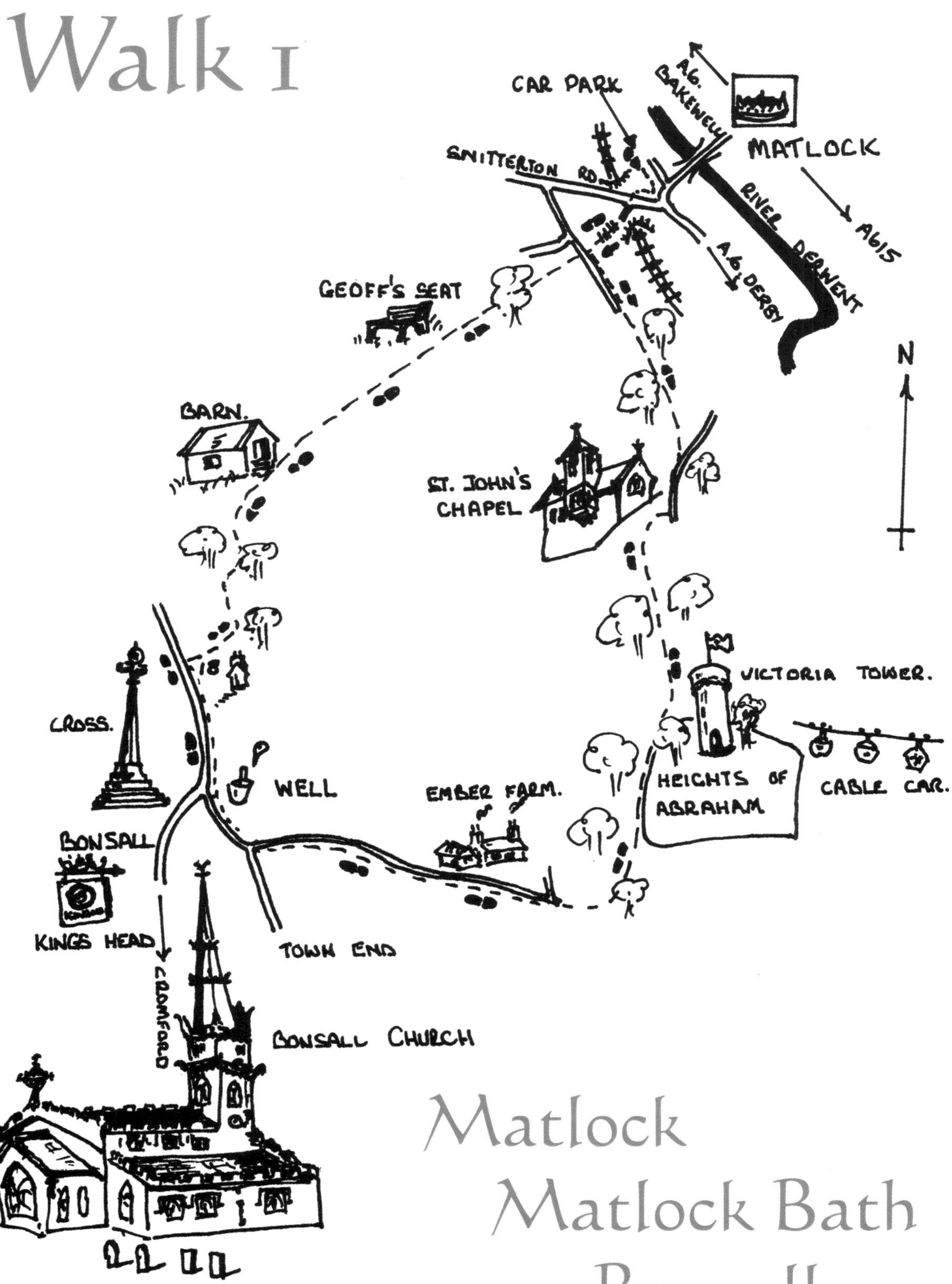

Matlock
Matlock Bath
Bonsall

Walk 1

Matlock - Matlock Bath - Bonsall

About this walk

With many points of interest on the route, this walk starts in the picturesque setting of Matlock and takes you through the ancient village of Bonsall. A very attractive and varied walk, with sweeping, expansive views from the higher ground.

Distance	6.7km 4.2 miles
Terrain	There is a steady ascent from Matlock for most of the first half of this walk but after this stage the way is either level or downhill. Parts of the route can be wet and muddy after rainy periods. A very varied terrain, including fields, tracks, lanes and footpaths.
Map	OS Explorer OL24 The Peak District, White Peak area. 1:25 000 scale.
Starting Point	The large car park by Matlock Railway Station and close to the bridge (off the A6(T)). This car park is free at time of writing. Grid reference SK 297 601.
Refreshments	Matlock offers a variety of pubs, cafés and shops. On the route is the Kings Head in Bonsall which serves meals and snacks. In season, the Heights of Abraham sells ice-cream and drinks to non ticket holders.

1. From car park entrance, walk to main road A6(T), turn *right*, walk a few paces and turn *right* again, into **Snitterton Road**. Cross road and walk up hill

2. Very shortly, where buildings end on right-hand side of road, take lane going up on left towards **Bridge Farm** (lane crosses railway line)

3. On reaching **Bridge Farm**, carry straight on up steps (do not follow lane going left)

4. Go through stile and follow path as it goes up and bears slightly right

✓ **The large Derbyshire Council building is clearly visible from here. Until the 1950s this was a centre for Hydrotherapy treatment, the largest of many in Matlock. It was built by John Smedley and was tremendously successful, with over 2,000 visitors a year. During the 2nd World War it was used for military purposes and was finally taken over by Derbyshire County Council.**

5. At top of path, go through stile in wall ahead and onto lane. Turn *left* (ignore path straight ahead) and walk up lane

✓ **Riber Castle lies over to the left. This was built by John Smedley as his private residence in 1862 at a cost of £60,000. After his wife's death it became a prep school, a food store during the war and finally a small zoo.**

6. Just past wall on right and before lane bends right towards farm, turn *left* and go through gap by large gate. Carry on down (wall on left)

7. As wall ends, keep following path as it goes right and then shortly bears left

8. Continue along and when path meets wall, turn *right*. Go over and through (a double) stile and continue down path

9. On meeting lane, turn *right* and go up hill

✓ **The unusual building on your right is St. John's Chapel of ease (a dependent church, built for people who lived a long way from the main church). It was built in 1897, at the expense of Louisa Harris, who lived at 'The Rocks', just below. She did this for the benefit of her relatives, who lived some distance from St. Giles' church, Matlock.**

10. As lane reaches house entrance, (ignore track to left) turn *right* up path by gateway

11. At top of path, bear left between walls and follow path as it winds through wooded area

12. Go up a few stone steps and follow path as it goes up

13. Cross stile (buildings on left) and continue along path

14. At gateway, go through stile and turn *right* (keep wall on right)

✓ **The tower in view on the left is named after Princess (later Queen) Victoria, who visited Matlock Bath in 1832. Work on the tower was begun in 1844 by the then owner of the Heights of Abraham. It is 800 feet above sea level and about 50 feet in height.**

15. At top of field, go over stile by gateway and carry on up. Pass through stone gateposts and continue up

16. Go over next stile by gateway (ignore paths to left and right) and carry on up

Kings Head, Bonsall

17. Just above (private!) entrance to **Heights of Abraham**, go over stile in wall on *left*

✓ **The Heights of Abraham were named by an army officer in the 18th century. He was struck by their similarity to the wooded slopes where General Wolfe's battle was fought in Quebec.**

18. Follow path down alongside grounds of **Heights of Abraham**

19. Cross surfaced road and continue through wooded area (this path will continue for some distance)

20. At end of path, go through stone stile and turn *right* up track (past **Ember Farm**)

21. Go through gateway, turn *left* and walk up lane

✓ **Dene Quarry (previously Dene Hollow) at Cromford is visible in the distance on the left. This produces crushed limestone rock for roadstone and concrete.**

22. Continue to follow lane down to **Bonsall**. In front of church, turn *right* and follow lane down into village

✓ **The Kings Head Inn, established 1677, shows the head of King Charles 11, rather than Charles 1, whom the title usually commemorates. The village cross is the tallest in Derbyshire. The first date on it is 1620 and could be the date it was repaired. Note interesting map and info board by telephone box.**

23. Go past cross and straight on up **High Street**. Between house numbers 28 (large red brick house) and 30, turn right and follow path up

24. At top of path go through stile and continue up field, heading <u>straight up</u> towards trees (ignore any paths to left or right)

25. At top of field, enter trees, go through stile and turn *left* along track

26. Carry on up track, with wall both sides (ignore all paths off)

27. At end of track, on reaching 'T-junction', turn *right* and go up hill

28. As this track meets another, turn *left*, head up a few paces and go over stile by large gate, attached to tree (ignore other gate to right). Continue up (ignore all paths off)

29. As track widens slightly and curves right, go a <u>little</u> further and through stile on right

30. With your back to stile, walk diagonally left towards boundary wall and left-hand barn

31. Continue along field, passing stone barn (on left) and keeping wall on right (ignore other barn over to right)

32. Go through stile ahead and straight on across field (mound of underground reservoir visible on right)

33. Go through stile in wall opposite, cross lane and through stile on other side of lane

34. Head slightly right across field and cross stile in wall on right (stile not immediately visible)

35. Turn *left* and walk down hill (wall on left). Follow path as it goes through ruined wall and gradually bears right, away from left hand wall

✓ **Excellent view of Matlock ahead (on good days!).**

36. At bottom right corner of field, go through gate and turn *right* onto lane

37. Very shortly, turn *left*, cross stile and head down field (wall on left)

38. At bottom of field, go through stile, head diagonally right across next field and through stile by gate in lower right-hand corner

39. Cross lane and go through stile opposite (farm on right)

40. Head down left-hand side of field, through stile at bottom and continue straight down. Shortly, go through opening in small ruined wall

41. Continue on and soon, by small wall on left, go through (indistinct) stile near gateway and head straight down right-hand side of field (wall or trees on right)

42. Go through narrow stile and straight on, down right-hand side of next field

43. At bottom of this field, go through stile ahead and again follow path down right-hand side of field

44. Go over stile on right, just before bottom of field, then shortly through further stile and continue down on right

45. Pass through stone gateposts, cross stile ahead and turn immediately *right*

46. Cross over lane, go through stile and head down hill

47. Go through further stile, down steps and straight on (past **Bridge Farm**). On meeting **Snitterton Road**, turn *right* and continue down to main road **A6(T)**. Turn *left* and very shortly turn *left* again to return to car park

St. John's Chapel

Walk 2

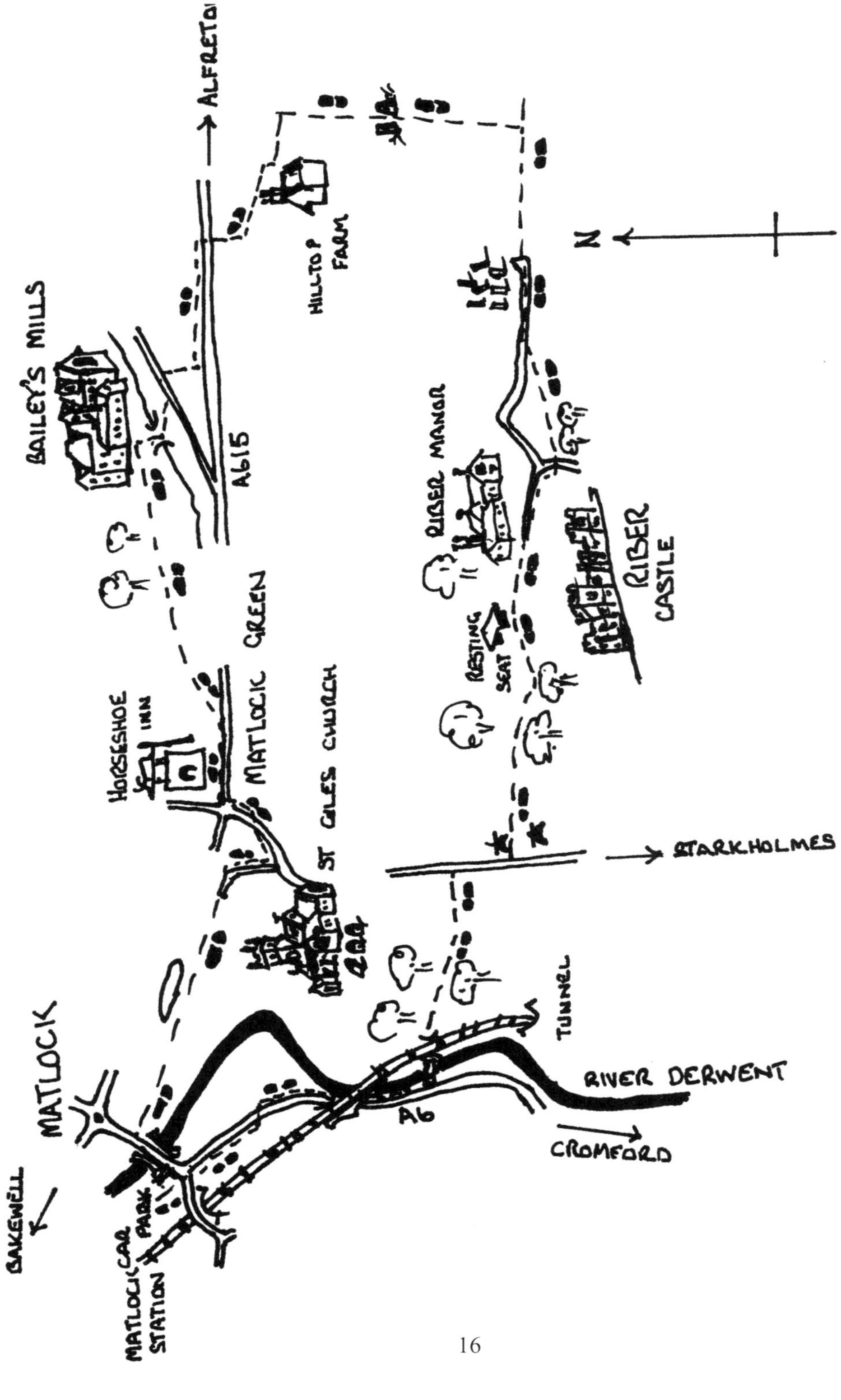

ALFRETON
BAILEY'S MILLS
HILLTOP FARM
A615
MATLOCK GREEN
HORSESHOE INN
ST GILES CHURCH
RIBER MANOR
RIBER CASTLE
RESTING SEAT
N
STARKHOLMES
MATLOCK
BAKEWELL
MATLOCK CAR PARK STATION
TUNNEL
RIVER DERWENT
A6
CROMFORD

Walk 2

Matlock - Riber Castle - Matlock Cliff

About this walk

This route takes you through 'old' and 'new' Matlock and up to the fascinating Riber Castle. Built as a private residence in the 19th century, it has stunning views over the town and surrounding countryside. This is not a long walk and well worth the climb out of the town up to Riber. An interesting mix of town and countryside with ample opportunities to drink in the landscape.

Distance	6km 3.7 miles
Terrain	The initial walk up to Riber Castle is slightly strenuous but it is well worth stopping occasionally to take in the view behind you. From this point the way is fairly level or downhill. There is a good mix of paths, tracks, fields and pavements. Some areas can be slightly uneven and muddy underfoot.
Map	OS Explorer OL24 The Peak District, White Peak area. 1:25 000 scale.
Starting Point	The large car park by Matlock Railway Station and close to the bridge (off the A6(T)). This car park is free at time of writing. Grid reference SK 297 601.
Refreshments	Matlock offers a variety of pubs, cafés and shops.

1. From car park entrance, head to main road A6(T) and walk along this road (shops on both sides)

2. A little further on, cross road on zebra crossing and then continue on past shops and under railway bridge

✓ *Note the shape of the last house before bridge, at the end of Holt Terrace!*

3. Continue to walk beside **River Derwent** and take first bridge across on your left

4. Pass under railway bridge and continue up. As path meets lane, bear left

5. As lane meets road, cross and turn *right* to head up hill

6. On reaching main entrances of schools on left, take track between them (to right of driveway of first school)

7. At top of track, go through stile and follow path up right-hand side of field (this soon becomes paved)

8. At top of field, go through stile, bear left up hill and continue along paved path

9. Go through stile and continue up, past cottage on left and outbuildings on right

✓ *Riber Castle was built in 1862 by John Smedley, owner of a large hydrotherapy establishment in Matlock. This was his private residence, constructed at a cost of £60,000. After his wife's death, it became a prep school, a food store during the war and finally a small zoo.*

10. On coming to end of path, go through stile and continue up track

11. Where track meets lane, turn *left* down lane

12. As lane meets junction (by **Riber Manor** on left) turn *right*

✓ Riber Manor is dated 1633, probably built on the site of an earlier house. Close by, a little further along the lane, lies Riber Hall, dated 1661. These days it is a rather up-market hotel.

13. Very shortly, go over stile on left and then slightly diagonally across to wall on left. Go through stile a little way down wall

14. From stile, turn *right* and walk down right-hand side of field

15. At bottom of field, go through stile and turn *right* along lane (ignore stile almost opposite)

16. At end of lane, go straight on past house on right and over stile straight ahead

17. As wall ends on left, turn *left* along wide grassy area

18. On meeting wall, go through stile and across field to opposite wall (past two stone posts)

19. Continue through stile and bear slightly right towards stile in wall opposite

20. Go over this stile and across field, again bearing slightly right to wall opposite

21. Go through stile and continue down a few paces and at corner of wall, turn *left*

22. On reaching farm track, walk a short way and then turn *right* through stile by stone gateway (farm entrance on left)

Riber Manor

23. From stile, turn immediately *left* and follow path across hill (farmhouse on left)

24. Pass through stile in wall ahead, then slightly right and through stile in opposite wall

25. Go across to next wall, through gate in right-hand corner and turn *right* down hill

26. After a few paces, go through further gate and walk down track (wall on both sides)

27. Cross road and turn *left* along pavement (for approx. 250m)

28. Where houses begin, go through gap in wall on right, down steps and follow path

✓ Bailey's Mills, ahead of you, date from the 17th century. They were originally powered by water wheels, later by steam, and were bought by the Bailey family around 1800. Used as flour mills from 1866, the top mill included a malt house. Malt was in great demand at the time, not least for home brewed beer!

29. In front of mill, turn *left* up road, then almost immediately *right* down track

30. By wall and gateway of apartments, go straight on through small gateway and up path

31. After a few paces, turn *left* (ignore paths ahead and to right)

32. At end of path, go through stile and straight to main road. Turn *right* along pavement, and head towards **Matlock** town

33. On reaching **The Horseshoe Inn**, cross to other side of road (pelican crossing just beyond inn, if preferred)

34. Go up **Church Street** (road directly opposite inn) and cross this road to be on right-hand pavement

35. Continue up hill to **St. Giles' Church**

✓ St. Giles' Church stands on a hill overlooking Matlock with some fine views of the Derwent Valley. The church is ancient but was substantially rebuilt in the 19th century. It has a Norman font, some fine stained glass windows and memorials to the Wolley family of Old Riber Hall. The Matlock War Memorial is also here, built on high ground above the church.

✓ This area is the older part of the parish and was the original Matlock, with several houses dating from the 17th century. Amongst the local people buried in the churchyard are a considerable number of tombstones belonging to those who did not survive their treatment in the many Hydros (this is also true of other local churchyards).

36. Just before the church, turn *right* down steep lane

37. At bottom of lane (after bridge) turn *left* along quiet road and head straight on into park. Follow path through park (river on left)

38. On leaving park, cross road and turn *left* over bridge to return to car park on right

Walk 3

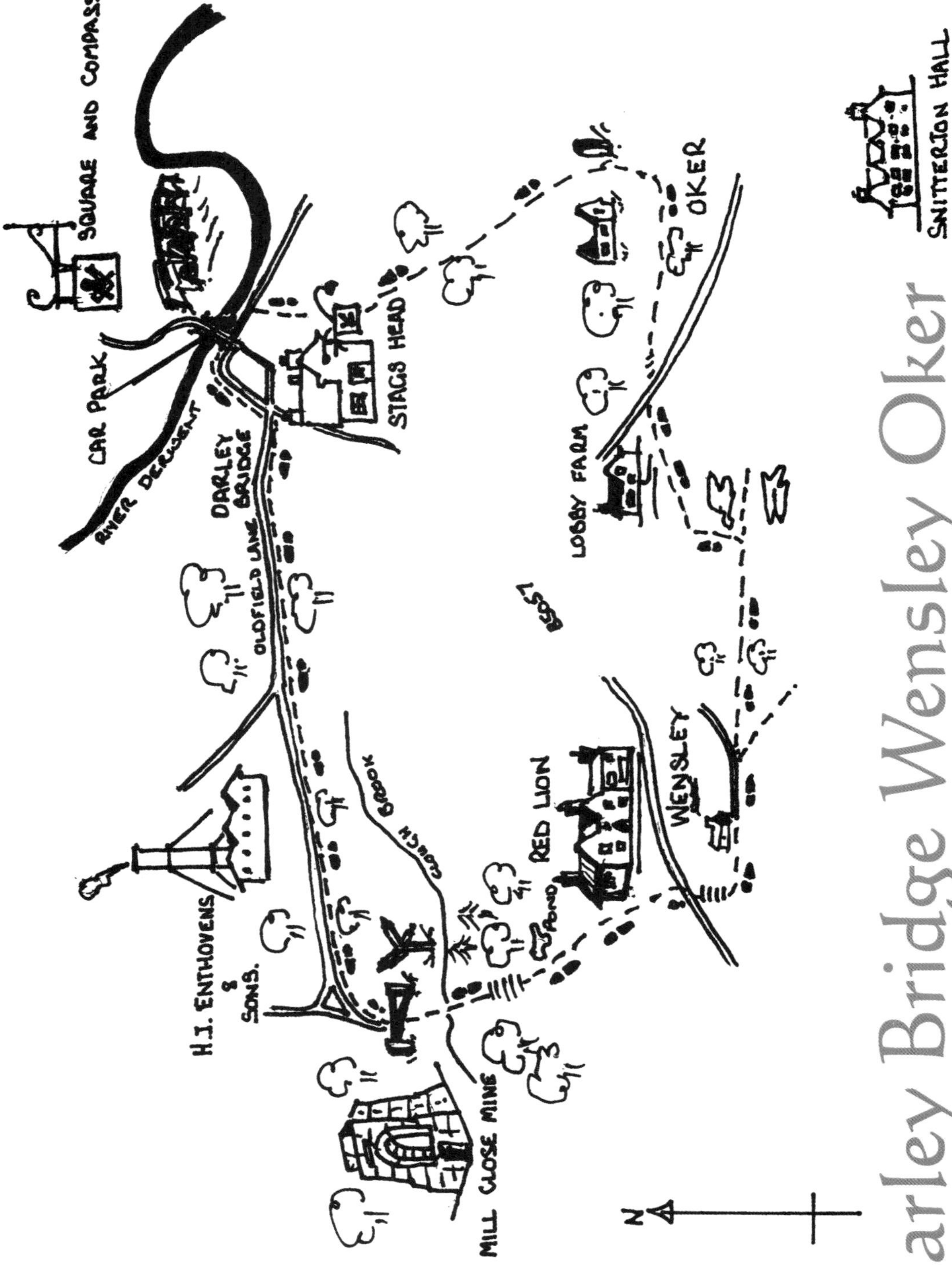

Darley Bridge Wensley Oker

Walk 3

Darley Bridge - Wensley - Oker

About this walk

A very attractive walk, affording good views over the countryside from the various high points. A nice blend of village and countryside, steeped in lead mining history. Short enough to consider as a relaxed late afternoon or evening walk.

Distance 5.4km   3.4 miles

Terrain A fairly short walk which is not too demanding. There is one steepish ascent from the footbridge up into Cambridge Wood, which is rough underfoot. A mixture of footpaths, tracks, fields, rural road and pavements. Can be muddy in places, although generally sound.

Map OS Explorer OL24 The Peak District, White Peak area. 1:25 000 scale.

Starting Point Approaching Darley Bridge from Darley Dale on B5057 (off A6), cross bridge (over River Derwent) and turn left immediately for parking spaces. Grid reference SK 270 620.

Refreshments Three Stags Heads in Darley Bridge.

1. From parking area, walk back towards bridge, cross road and turn *left*

2. Shortly, just before **Three Stags Heads**, turn *right* into **Oldfield Lane**

3. At top of hill, as road bears slightly right, turn *left* up lane

✓ The Enthoven Company deals in lead recycling and is the largest single site producer of recycled lead in Europe. Lead has been mined on this site since Roman times. The current site was originally the Mill Close Mine, one of the most valuable lead mines in Great Britain. The smelter sits at the centre of a 250 acre woodland site, which has been recognised by English Nature as a Site of Special Scientific Interest. The estate has been naturally forested for centuries and is home to a large variety of wildlife.

4. Approximately 300m further on, ignore stile on left. Later, as lane bends sharply to right (small grassy island in road), turn *left* and pass through gap at side of metal gate

5. Take lower track heading down hill and follow this as it curves down

✓ The stone remains up on the right (partly hidden by foliage in summer), formed part of Watt's Shaft, belonging to Mill Close Mine. The building contained the engine and pumping equipment. Pumping was vital as the mine was subject to flooding. This was once the richest lead mine in Britain, producing a third of the country's output. Mill Close Mine, which had been worked for centuries, reached its peak in the 1930s, employing around 800 men, before mining operations ceased in 1940.

6. Ignore first path off to right. Take second path a few paces on, as track curves left

7. Just a few steps down this, turn sharp *left* down path, leading to footbridge across stream

8. Cross footbridge and follow path round, up hill into wooded area

9. Continue to follow path up hill, passing small pond on left

10. Near top of hill, go up a few steps, over stile and continue up left-hand side of field

11. Ignore gateway on left, and carry on down to bottom of field (keep to left-hand side)

12. Go down steps in left-hand corner of field, through narrow gap in wall, cross road and turn *right*

✓ **Wensley is mentioned in the Domesday Book as "Wodnesleie", meaning the "clearing dedicated to Woden" the god of war. In the 18th and 19th centuries, many of the villagers would have been employed in the lead mining industry in the fields around the village and Winster.**

13. After a few paces, turn *left* through stone stile (and gate), head down steps and along path

14. Follow main path, as it winds down to bottom and through small gateway

15. After gateway, turn *left*, continue past cottages and follow track down

16. Shortly after cottages, as lane starts to rise, turn *right* and head down hill along path (ignore path on right going up hill). Depending on season, the route may be wide and grassy or narrow and overgrown

✓ **Matlock in view ahead.**

17. Go through stile by gateway and continue down

18. After a few minutes, on approaching large rocky hillock on each side of the valley (with wall across path in sight) turn *left* and go through stile in wall

19. Head straight up rise and then bear right towards stile in middle of right-hand wall

20. Go through stile, then head to further stile in top left-hand corner of facing wall

21. Walk diagonally up hill towards farm. Enter farmyard through stile by gate, at higher side of farm buildings

✓ **To the right of you, on the horizon, lies Riber Castle. It was built in 1862 by John Smedley, owner of a large hydrotherapy establishment in Matlock. This was his private residence, constructed at a cost of £60,000. After his wife's death, it became a prep school, a food store during the war and finally a small zoo.**

22. Walk through farmyard and up to road. Cross road and go through stile almost opposite. Follow path as it heads up hill and bears right

23. Continue, as path passes small building on left and then houses on right. Follow it up into wooded area

24. At top of path, cross stile and turn *right*

25. Follow path down and shortly, as path forks left away from fence, follow it up hill

26. At top of hill, on leaving wooded area, turn *right* and follow path along ridge

✓ **Towards the end of ridge, note Snitterton Hall in the distance, on the right. There has been a manor house there since medieval times, probably built by the Snitterton Family. John Milward, one of the many owners and a colonel for the King in the Civil War, built the hall as we see it today, in the 17th century.**

27. At end of ridge, continue to follow path as it bears left and goes down

28. At bottom of ridge, where path meets track, turn *left*

29. Follow track up hill, past derelict building and stone post

30. Continue up through line of trees and then follow straight on

✓ **Darley Bridge lies straight ahead and Darley Dale is on its right across the valley. The Peak Railway line runs along the valley and steam trains can regularly be seen at weekends and holidays.**

31. At fork in path just inside wooded area, turn *right* (do not go through stone gateposts ahead)

32. Follow path down (valley and villages on right), go over stile in line of trees and continue

33. Go past houses on right and along lane ahead, passing through stile at side of gate

34. Shortly after, turn *right* over stile and head down field

35. At bottom, cross stile and small stream and continue straight on across field (ignore stile on left)

36. Cross stile at bottom left-hand corner, turn *left* and return to car parking area

The Bakewell Walks

Edensor Village

Bakewell Pudding Shop

Rutland Arms

Park in Bakewell

Bakewell

Bakewell - This market town was mentioned in the Domesday Book as 'Badequella', meaning Bath-well, a reference to the mineral springs that exist in the area. There are still two springs in existence, one in Bath Street, and Holywell in the recreation grounds. Every August the wells are 'dressed' in a ceremony which probably dates back to pagan times.

Bakewell is situated on the River Wye, which is crossed here by a 13th century five arched bridge. The town now lies in the Peak District National Park. In 924 Edward the Elder had a fortified town built here, at a point where the river was fordable. Bakewell has one of the oldest markets in the area. The first recorded market was held in 1254 and they still take place every Monday.

There are numerous old inns offering refreshments in interesting surroundings.

Bakewell Pudding - The famous pudding was invented accidentally at the White Horse Inn (now Rutland Arms Hotel) in the 1860s. A cook misinterpreted instructions and poured egg mixture over the jam instead of mixing it in the pastry. What should have been a tart became a pudding. Puddings made to the original recipe can be bought at several shops in the town centre.

Haddon Hall - is just south of Bakewell. There has been a dwelling on this site since the 11th century, but the present house dates from the late 12th century. In 1703 the Manners family moved to Belvoir Castle in Leicestershire and Haddon Hall fell into disrepair and was abandoned. The 9th Duke of Rutland devoted his life to restoring the house, which is a very fine example of a Medieval and Tudor country house, and is well worth a visit. The Hall also has an outstanding garden and offers a restaurant and gift shop. Tel 01629 812855.

The Old House Museum - is in the old Tax Collector's house. The building dates from the reign of Henry VIII but was later converted into mill workers' accommodation by Sir Richard Arkwright, who established Lumford cotton spinning mill in 1777 and put his son in charge. The museum houses 14 beamed rooms including a draper's shop, a Victorian kitchen, a wheelwright and a smithy. Other rooms have Ashford Marble, lace, toys, china and photographs. It is open from 1st April until the end of October from 1.30pm (11am in July and August) to 4pm. Guides are always at hand to answer questions and the museum also organizes talks and visits. Tel 01629 813165 for more information.

The Bakewell Show - takes place on the first Wednesday and Thursday of August on land adjoining the Agricultural Centre. The first local show took place in 1819. It is now a major agricultural and horticultural event with all sorts of animals being shown along with show jumping and exhibitions of local crafts and produce.

Tourist Information is in the Old Market Hall Bridge Street.

The Mill Owner's Tale

Father's funeral took place yesterday. Great pomp and ceremony there was, upwards of two thousand people lining the streets. All those heads bowed in silence as the black carriage passed by, some people even weeping. "You must feel so proud," an elderly man says to me, "a great man, that was, a very great man - brought well-being to thousands. And of course you, sir," he adds diplomatically, "are clearly following in his footsteps."

I'm unsure about that. I prefer to think of myself as my own man, but the sons of famous fathers can rarely attain that state. All the more difficult in my case, bearing his name - Richard - and following in the same business. It saddens me to say I was never close to him, although I am his only son and have but one half-sister. He was too enthralled by his work to be close to any human being, and that almost certainly included my mother. Did she die of purely physical causes, just a few months after my birth, thirty-seven years ago? Or was there just so little love, so little encouragement to stay alive? Many women die in childbirth, or soon after, you may well remind me. Perhaps my suspicions do him an injustice. It may be that she was taken by a fever, that she had not the strength to recover from a difficult birth. Perhaps the blow to him was so great, it put a coldness in his heart towards me. We never spoke of it. As a part of my early childhood, I remember him hardly at all. Later, he spoke to me only of cotton, of the mills, the machines, the workers. Of these I learned a great deal from my youth, and of course thanks to him I have long enjoyed wealth and lived in comfort. But never have I played the role of spoilt, incompetent son. In all honesty, I have a true mind for business and a sound enough judgement. Even he, who loved to have all things within his control, recognised that. He had no qualms about leaving me almost everything. I have long proved my worth to him and indeed I do not now intend to squander his work or his fortune. Riches offer a far better life than poverty, and I desire that my children enjoy good lives also.

Unlike my father, I have a large family. I feel such affection for every one of them that it is a puzzle to me that he could show so little affection for me. But as I have already indicated, he was not a man of feeling, and nothing counted for him as greatly as his work. My poor stepmother must have discovered this to her cost, and despite bearing him three daughters - of whom only my sister, Susannah, survives - she left him, and has now for some years lived with Susannah and her family. For the last few years of his life, my father was alone. I have to admit that I have seen him rarely during these recent times. The days were gone when I felt the need to consult him on business matters, and his views, which he always expressed in a greatly overbearing way, were not always my own.

I have not shed tears for him, but I shall ensure that the family honours his memory, and that what he gave to Cromford, to Bakewell, indeed to England, is not lost. He came from nothing, or at least from precious little. Youngest of a big family, no schooling, barely able to read and write - yet he gave to England a way of industry that is now making us great throughout the world. Never before in history has cotton, or anything else, been produced in such vast quantities under one roof. Of course, there are those who mourn the old ways, the cottage ways, but they will not return. My father has led the country to a different future.

Yes, of course it's all been so much easier for me, though he was a severe task master and had I not shown ability and usefulness he would, be assured, have quickly dispensed with my services. He was not a man to feel loyalty, if it went against the interests of his business. Friends, who had helped him in the past - lent him money, joined him as partners in various enterprises - were dropped promptly if he felt it advantageous to do so. 'Friends' is perhaps the wrong word, for a man like my father had use only for allies. Friends would always become an inconvenience. Several have, in the end, felt venomous towards him and probably with good cause.

I suppose, now, that Mary and I will leave Bakewell and move to Rock House in Cromford. The Cromford Works are larger than Lumford Mill, and I feel it right to be near them, though I confess I will miss this town greatly. Father set me up here fourteen years ago, and my mill has done wonders for the place. It was nothing but a poor and shabby village until then, held together by a few impoverished hill farmers and lead miners. It boasted nothing but a decent boys' school, set up by Lady Manners over a century ago. Nowadays the place can hold its head up.

I know that Mary has no wish to live in Rock House - father's old home, with its large window overlooking the mill, so that he could watch all the goings-on. Once Willersley Castle is finished, we will no doubt move in there - a huge mansion of a place, started by Father in his desire to show something for his wealth, but not finished in time for him. Of course, I understand my wife's reluctance. She knew father never approved of her, and indeed his words to both of us were scathing when our first child, Elizabeth, was born just four weeks after our wedding. No doubt he suspected Mary of seducing me, in order to secure a life of wealth, but if that were indeed the case, then what of it? I am content enough. He treated her, thereafter, with some scorn - an attitude that did nothing to improve my own relationship with him. And he has always seemed to take as little interest in his grandchildren as he once did in me.

Mary and I have eight children, six boys and two girls. She is happy, though I shall be pleased enough to see more. The Arkwright name is safe with me! Large families seem to me to be an altogether good and natural thing. Generally they are unavoidable in any case! Who would choose to lead a life of abstinence? Certainly I would not, but fortunately Mary is not the type of woman to suggest it. So I am confident there will be more. Of course, there is great risk in childbirth, especially if a woman is delicate in health. Thank God, Mary is strong and has always recovered quickly.

The mill women, too, seem sturdy and robust on the whole, and of course it is to a working family's advantage to produce many offspring, because each child can bring in good money. A family with six or more working children is obviously going to be far better off than one with two! Father always favoured employing whole families, but neither of us has ever taken orphaned or destitute children from the workhouses, even though they can provide almost free labour. Other mill owners have fewer scruples, especially up in Lancashire, when new mills seem to be opening up almost by the week. If a hundred children can be shipped up from a London workhouse, and then worked till they drop for nothing but a meagre bit of food and a couple of blankets, then it's a very fine profit to the owner, isn't it? It's even worthwhile for him to agree to take on a couple of imbecile children along with every twenty sound ones.

I would never do such a thing. Father, to give him his due, rarely set a child on to work below the age of eight and insisted they had a bit of schooling first. His rule has always been that a child must be able to read a bit before starting work, though in honesty that rule is broken often enough. And usually it's broken because the child's parents will plead with us to take it on, able to read or not. Most parents can see no benefit to reading - not for children facing a working life in the mills.

Obviously my own children are in a quite different position. I intend to send all the boys to Eton, and thereafter to Cambridge. I desire that they feel completely at ease among people of wealth and rank. Father never felt such ease. Even when he was made Sheriff of Derbyshire five years ago, in 1787, and a little later became 'Sir' Richard, he expressed contempt for the aristocracy and never wished to associate with them. A poor childhood in Preston, without schooling, followed by apprenticeship as a barber, ill prepared him for an exchange of social graces! He was horrified to learn recently that I have lent the Duchess of Devonshire a significant sum of money, to cover her gambling debts. But I am well aware of the benefits of good connections.

But as for the large, hard-working families who serve us at Bakewell, and of course at Cromford, they have much to be grateful for. Men are employed as machine makers and repairers, and of course as overseers. Women and children work at the carding and spinning machines in our water-powered cotton mills. Father's famous water frame, perhaps the greatest technical advance of our time, is simple enough to be handled by a reasonably attentive child. I have always believed that he invented it, though others have claimed he stole the design, along with several more. Whatever the truth, no one ever made it work as he did, on such a scale, to such great profit. Even his enemies would have to admit he was the greatest industrialist in the world. Cromford has attracted families from miles around and many of them live in the good, sound houses that he had built for them. There's now a regular market, a church and a good-sized hostelry - the Black Greyhound. Working children are sent to Sunday School, boys one Sunday and girls the next. Is that not better than old lead mining families scratching a paltry living, in what was a desolate spot, offering nothing?

And here in Bakewell, as in other towns, it's much the same. Lumford Mill has provided plenty of work and this tiny place has grown beyond imagination since it was set up. Mary and I are treated with much respect in the town. I've got around three hundred and fifty workers, mostly women and children - there's less need for men, except as overseers, as we do little machine making here. But I've still built over fifty dwellings, and charge them out at a low rent. I'm particularly pleased with the cottages in New Square - the centre of the town now looks respectable and solid, and there's many a pleasant night to be had at the White Horse Inn. I know a good many of my workers by name. Not a bad lot, they are, though they need to be kept at their task. That's where the overseers come in. One woman has suggested to me that she, and other women, could fulfil such a role! That did amuse me. Women, by nature, will gossip and fritter away their time. Their fingers are nimble enough - better than a man's - but they can hardly be placed in a position of authority. The men would take it as an insult also.

Working shifts are certainly not overly long - twelve hours a day, six days a week - a lot better than some of the mills further north. There's a day and a night shift, of course - the machines are kept running continuously, though younger children generally only work the days. Two shifts are a boon to a lot of families. It means fewer beds are needed in their small houses and that gives people much more space to move around in.

Altogether, our workers have much reason to feel content and grateful, and judging by the turn out yesterday, most of them do. Up in Lancashire, there have been problems over the last few years - machines are getting smashed up by mobs, mills have even been set on fire. Father lost a brand new mill in Chorley that way. Do they really believe that without machines there would be work for all of them? As I said, the old days of cottage spinning will soon be gone for good. In any case, the population is now too great to be supported in that way. There are hordes of children everywhere you look, and their bellies are most likely to be filled through the efforts of people like my father and myself. Of course, father was very fearful for Cromford after that Chorley affair. He had a cannon set up to defend it, and plenty of arms and trained men at the ready, but we've had no trouble around here. People know there's far worse fates than working for Arkwright Mills!

If your wanderings take you round the town of Bakewell, spare a thought for my efforts, which helped to make the place handsome and prosperous. The town is now, of course, nothing more than a picturesque souvenir, a place for spending wealth, not creating it. The real world, the world of manufacture, moved away from here, as it did from Cromford, many years ago. It is the tourist, not the worker, who is important now.

Perhaps the lives of the Arkwright workers would seem dreary and unrelenting to your mind. But there is certainly no ill in hard work, and their children did not starve. My own conscience is quite clear.

Bakewell Old Market Hall, now Tourist Information Centre
Photograph – by kind permission of Matlock Local Studies Library

Walk 4

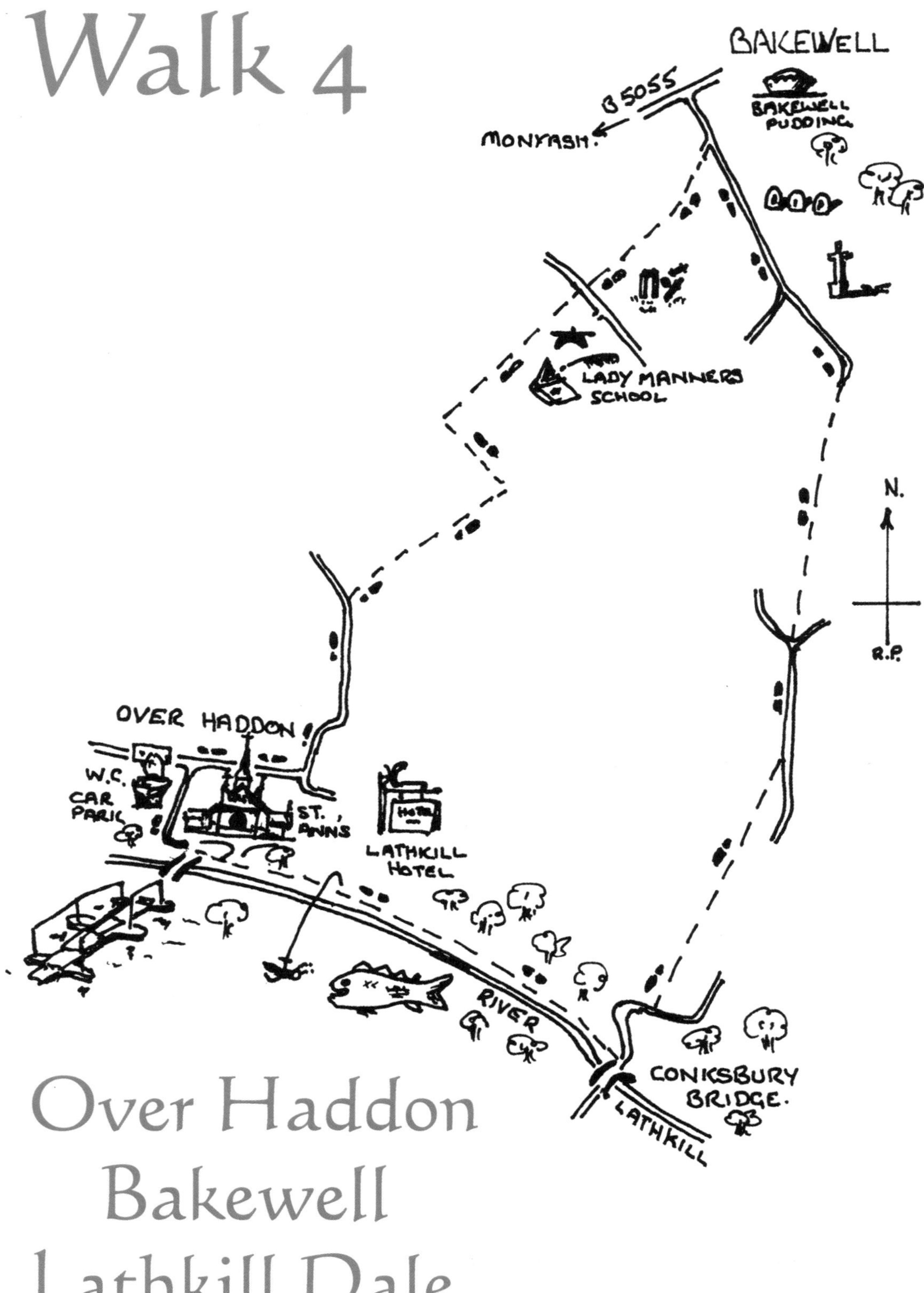

Over Haddon
Bakewell
Lathkill Dale

30

Walk 4

Over Haddon - Bakewell - Lathkill Dale

About this walk

This is a lovely walk, starting in the picturesque village of Over Haddon and offering the opportunity to visit the ancient market town of Bakewell, if desired. Over Haddon clings to the top of the steep side of the Lathkill Valley. You will pass through an attractive variety of meadows, dales and beautiful riverside. Lathkill Dale is a National Nature Reserve and is renowned for wild flowers, especially orchids, cowslips and the rare Jacob's Ladder.

Distance	7.2km 4.5 miles
Terrain	A mixture of pathways, tracks and some quiet roadways. Not a demanding walk and generally sound underfoot. It includes a few gradual rises, and one longer and steeper pull at the end, from the riverside back up into Over Haddon (a number of benches along this road if a breather is needed).
Map	OS Explorer OL24 The Peak District, White Peak area. 1:25 000 scale.
Starting Point	Over Haddon car park off B5055 Bakewell to Monyash road, (pay and display). Public toilets in car park. Grid reference SK 203 664.
Refreshments	Over Haddon has a 'diner' with limited opening times, serving various refreshments and also the Lathkil Hotel. Bakewell has a variety of shops, pubs, teashops and restaurants.

1. From main car park entrance, turn *right* and follow road up (**Main Street**)

2. As houses end, follow road as it bears left (it now becomes **Bakewell Road**)

3. Continue as road bears right then left (ignore turn to right to **Youlgrave**)

4. As road again bends sharply left, go through stile in wall on right

5. Follow path down (wall on right), go over gated stile in wall ahead and turn *right*

6. Go through stile by gateway and head down through wide gateway, to bottom left-hand corner of field

7. Continue down (wall on left), then go through further stile and carry on (wall still on left)

8. As wall bends to left, go through double gated stile in wall on left (if you meet the road, you've missed the stile!)

9. From here, bear very slightly left, then follow wall on right-hand side (going past small farm outbuilding against wall)

10. At top of field cross stile in corner near gateway

11. As wall ends on right, go straight across field and on reaching other side, turn *right* (stay in same field) and head towards school buildings (**Lady Manners School**)

12. Go over stile in wall, turn *left* then almost immediately *right* (within same field). Keep heading towards school

✓ **Lady Manners School was founded in 1636 by Grace, Lady Manners, wife of George, Lord Manners of Haddon. In its early days it admitted boys only, to educate them in 'good learning and Christian religion'. The school deed stipulated that the schoolmaster was to remain unmarried, and 'if the said Schoolemaister shall at any time afterward marry, or shall live disorderly or scandalously, that then the said Schoolemaister shall have noe benefitt by the said Annuitie or rente charge, but shall be displaced from the said Schoole'.**

13. Go through gate and along path on left-hand side of school

14. On meeting road, cross straight over and head down passage (through school sports fields). Go through further gate and continue

15. As path meets pavement, head straight on down (past houses). As pavement curves right, cross road and head straight down passageway

16. Go through stile and continue down, as path becomes lane

✓ **The market town of Bakewall, which was mentioned in the Domesday Book, is situated on the River Wye in the Peak District National Park. The river is crossed by a 13th century five arched bridge. (see page 25 for more details of the town)**

17. As lane curves right, go straight on down steps to reach road

❖ **If you wish to visit Bakewall, turn left, and then right at next junction (town centre approximately five minutes). Come back to this point to continue walk. This road is called Yelo Road.**

18. Turn *right* and follow this road until it reaches cemetery, then take road along right-hand side of cemetery (**Burton Edge**)

19. As road bears right, head straight along track (passing school on right). Go through 2 stiles and continue on down (wall on left)

20. Pass through stile by small gate and carry on (wall on both sides)

21. Go through further stile by gateway and continue down (wall and derelict farm building on left)

22. Cross stream, turn *right* and follow path along (just in from stream on right)

23. Go through stile by gateway and keep to path as it bears left up hill

24. At top of incline, continue up field, bearing slightly diagonally right towards small gate in hedge

25. Go through this gate and bear left up hill (hedge on left). Continue to right-hand corner of field

26. Go over stile by gateway and walk diagonally right to far corner of field

27. Go through gate, turn *left* and walk beside road, passing farm on left and road on right. (This road leads to **Over Haddon** and car park if you need to cut the walk short, but you would miss an attractive riverside section)

28. Continue on and after a couple of minutes, as road starts to rise, go through stile in wall on right and straight across field to stile opposite

29. Go through this stile and then straight across very long field towards trees at bottom (ignore path crossing field later). You are heading for stile in wall at opposite end

✓ **View of Over Haddon village on right.**

30. Go through stile in wall and turn right down 'quiet lane'

31. Follow lane down as it bends left. As lane bends to right, turn sharp *right* through gate

✓ **Just before turning right, note Conksbury Bridge ahead, one of the oldest bridges in the area. On a steep bank overlooking it to the south, there was once a village, but this was abandoned during medieval times, soon after the bridge was built.**

32. Walk alongside **River Lathkill**. (You can relax and put the book away for a while, along this stretch!)

33. Eventually, as path ends (by stone footbridge) turn *right* between buildings, follow lane up hill and eventually back to car park

Walk 5

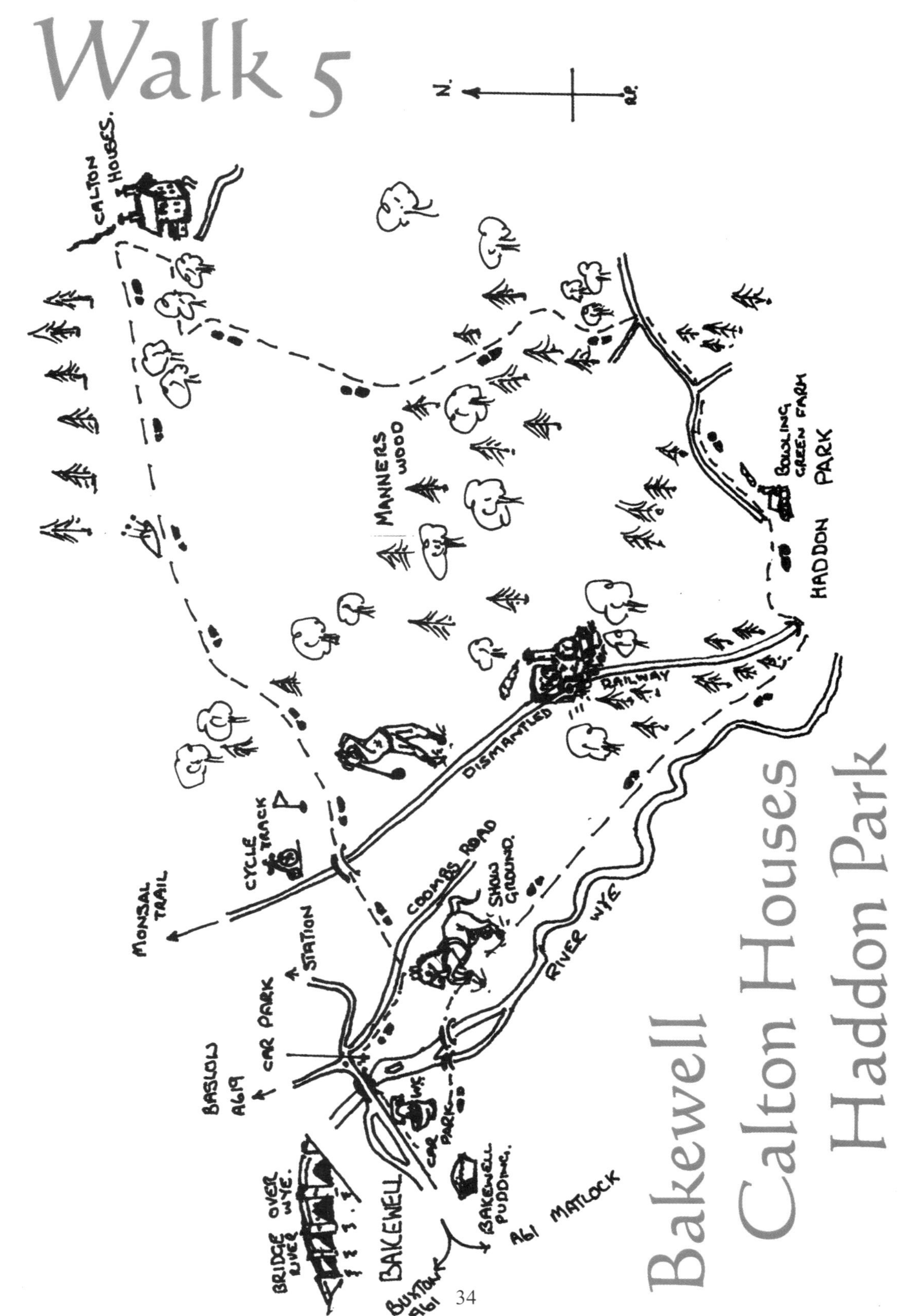

Bakewell
Calton Houses
Haddon Park

Walk 5

Bakewell - Calton Houses - Haddon Park

About this walk

This is a beautiful and varied walk. It starts and finishes in the ancient market town of Bakewell, which you can explore if you wish, but soon takes you into the picturesque Chatsworth and Haddon estates, with their rolling countryside, including farmland, woods and riverside. Lots of opportunities to enjoy the sight of wild flowers and birds.

Distance	9.5km 5.9 miles
Terrain	Near the start, going up through the wood from the golf course, there is a longish, fairly steep climb that is quite stony underfoot. Later there is a less steep and more gradual pull, but the remainder of the walk is fairly level or downhill. Likely to be muddy in places but generally sound underfoot.
Map	OS Explorer OL24 The Peak District, White Peak area. 1:25 000 scale.
Starting Point	Tourist Information Centre in Bridge Street, Bakewell. There are several car parks in and around the town. Toilets close to Tourist Information Centre and at end of walk by Agricultural Centre. Grid reference SK 218 685.
Refreshments	Bakewell is a bustling market town, offering a good number of cafés, restaurants, pubs and fish and chip shops (look out for the original Bakewell Pudding shops).

1. From Tourist Information Centre (**Bridge Street**) turn *right* (away from Rutland Arms, towards bridge). Walk across bridge

✓ **The River Wye, in the Peak District National Park, is crossed by this 13th century five arched bridge.**

2. From bridge, bear right into **Station Road** and then almost immediately turn *right* into **Coombs Road**

3. Walk along, and as houses end on right hand-side, cross road and go through wide double gate. Follow drive up

4. At top of drive, before houses, turn *right* through small gate by large one and walk on

5. As wide track bears left, go straight on along path (wall on right)

6. Cross stile by gate, go through further gate and over bridge

✓ **The footpath below the bridge was once part of the Midland Railway. The station in Bakewell closed in the 1960s, and the rails were taken up. This route has been converted into a long distance footpath and cycle track.**

7. Ignore stile on left (leads to old railway line) and continue on (be aware you are crossing a golf course here)

8. As path opens out onto golf course, follow it as it bears slightly left and up (around hillock) and carry on up into wood

9. Eventually, as path forks, carry straight on up (ignore concessionary path to right)

Old Postcard of Haddon Hall
Photograph – by kind permission of Matlock Local Studies Library

10. Near top, as path and track join, cross small stream and immediately turn *left*, then continue up towards edge of wood

11. Pass through small gate and bear diagonally right up hill

12. Follow path as it passes to right hand-side of small copse and continue straight on

13. Cross stile (pond on left) and then head straight on (keeping pond on left)

14. Very shortly, go over stile by gate on left, turn *right* and follow path down (fence on right)

15. Head towards gate at side of copse in distance. Go over stile by this gate and straight on (copse on right)

16. As path meets another (Swiss style cottage just ahead) turn *right* and follow path

17. On meeting wall, follow path as it bears right and down (wall on left)

18. A little further on, ignore gate on left and follow path as it bears right (wood on left)

19. As wall bends to left, go over stile by gate on left and continue along path as it bears left (wood on left)

20. Continue as path bears up right, away from wood and winds on up hill. Head for wood opposite, in distance

21. Go over stile (or 2 sets of gates) and follow path (from stile) straight on through wood (wall on right)

22. As wall ends, follow path as it turns left and then winds along

23. Emerge from wood through gateway and turn *left* (wall on left). Follow path for some time as it winds down through wood

24. Carry on down as path goes left, (ignore path to Haddon Estate woodland walk on right). Shortly, as path splits, bear right and continue down

25. Eventually, as path ends, ignore both lane turning sharp right and lane to left. Take lane carrying straight on.

26. As lane forks, bear right and continue along. Later ignore farm entrance on left and carry straight on

27. Very shortly, as lane bends to right, go straight ahead, down bridleway

✓ **The land and buildings on your left are part of the Haddon Hall Estate. Haddon Hall is a wonderful example of a medieval manor house. William the Conqueror's illegitimate son, Peverel, and his descendants held Haddon until it passed into the hands of the Vernon family in 1170. When Sir George Vernon died in 1567, the house passed to his son-in-law, Sir John Manners, son of the Earl of Rutland. The Hall is still one of the seats of the Dukes of Rutland and lies alongside the River Wye.**

28. Go through gate and straight on (railings on left). Pass through 2 further gates and walk on, following railings down

29. Pass through another gate and turn *left* down lane. Follow this lane down for some distance

30. As lane curves left (bridge now visible on left) turn right through small gate by large one and head up path

31. Continue as path goes along **River Wye**. Stay on path close to river

32. Path eventually leads down a few earth steps (house over on right). Continue along, go over stile and keep on alongside river

33. Cross small footbridge and continue as path moves away from river (hedge on right)

34. Continue on through gate ahead, then bear left to top left hand corner of field

35. Carry on, going through a number of gates and stiles

❖ **Another path runs parallel with this one on the other side of the hedge and it doesn't matter which one you take.**

36. Eventually you will reach Bakewell Agriculture Centre. From cattle grid, cross road and follow pavement (stream on left and Centre on right)

37. Cross bridge to immediate left of public toilets, then a further bridge to reach town centre

Walk 6

Calton Lees
Edensor
Chatsworth

Walk 6

Calton Lees - Edensor - Chatsworth

About this walk

This is a beautiful walk of long, sweeping views over the Chatsworth Estate and beyond. The whole experience is wonderfully relaxing, with its mixture of vast parkland and rural landscape. Adding a touch of grandeur is Chatsworth House, with its picturesque village of Edensor.

Distance	9.6km 6 miles
Terrain	This is not a demanding walk, for although it is uphill from shortly after the start to approximately half way, the ascent is easy and gradual, with stunning views. After the half way point, the walk is either downhill or level, other than a very short pull from the river up to the road. A lovely blend of meadows, paths, tracks, rural lanes and riverside. Parts of the walk may be muddy after rainy periods.
Map	OS Explorer OL24 The Peak District, White Peak area. 1:25 000 scale.
Starting Point	Calton Lees car park, just off B6012 immediately before entering Chatsworth Park from direction of Rowsley. Grid reference SK 258 685.
Refreshments	Garden centre café and toilets at beginning of walk. Edensor has Tea Rooms (with limited opening hours) and toilets, towards end of walk.

1. Turn *right* out of car park and follow road along

❖ **If you wish to visit Chatsworth Garden Centre and Café, take first lane on left (toilets here also).**

2. Continue on and follow as lane curves right past houses

3. As lane bends sharp left (towards **Rowsley**) continue straight on up track and through gateway (ignore private drive on right)

4. Follow this wide track for some distance and continue to follow as it goes through gateway and then between stone buildings (**Calton Houses**)

5. At top of track go through gateway, and turn *right* (wall on right)

6. Shortly, as wall bears to right, continue along path as bears slightly left (wood opposite)

7. Approximately $^2/_3$ of distance across field, turn *left* and follow path (wood now on right)

8. Continue up this path (woods visible on both sides)

9. Go over stile by gateway and carry on

10. At top of path, cross stile on left, turn *right* and head towards stile by pond

11. From this stile, bear slightly right (small copse on left) and follow path as it winds up and around hill

✓ **Bakewall is visible down in the valley on your left.**

12. Continue down as path becomes track and shortly go over stile by gateway. Carry on along track

13. Cross stile by large gateway, turn *right* and walk up lane

14. Eventually, as lane goes down and curves slightly left, bear right down wide track

15. As track joins another, carry straight on down (Edensor church steeple and, in the distance, the hunting tower of Chatsworth House, are both in view ahead)

✓ **The 16th century hunting tower may have been used for banqueting or as a summerhouse and probably by the ladies to watch the hunting in the park below. It is now let as holiday accommodation.**

16. Very shortly, walk through Edensor village

✓ **The small village of Edensor, pronounced 'Ensor', is in parkland owned by the Devonshire family, whose stately home, Chatsworth House, is nearby. Mentioned in the Domesday Book, Endsor originally lay between the river and the road through the Park. However, the fourth Duke of Devonshire, who had spent considerable money improving the House and gardens, decided to remove the buildings visible from the House. The sixth Duke completed the dismantling of the old village and built the present one.**

17. Go past church at other end of village and carry on down

❖ **If you wish to visit Edensor Tea Rooms and Post Office (toilets available here) turn right just after church.**

Old Mill, Chatsworth Park

✓ **Inside St. Peter's Church is a monument to the two sons of Bess of Hardwick (in Cavendish Chapel, just to right of alter). At the top of the churchyard is the grave of Kathleen Kennedy, sister of JF Kennedy, former President of the USA. She died in a plane crash shortly after her husband, Lord Hartington, had been killed in the Second World War.**

18. At end of village, go through iron gate by large gateway, cross road and head up path opposite

19. On meeting bridge (do not cross it), cross road, follow path down and across meadow

✓ **The original Chatsworth House was the work of Bess of Hardwick in the late 16th century, though no trace of this can now be seen. The first Duke rebuilt Chatsworth in Classical style between 1686 and 1707, with the Library and North Wing added by the sixth Duke between 1790 and 1858. The park was landscaped by the fourth Duke (1720-64), who engaged 'Capability' Brown to design the garden.**

20. At end of meadow, go up sandy path by **River Derwent** and carry on, keeping on path close to river

21. On reaching ruined mill on right, turn *right* and head up hill. Cross road by cattle grid, turn *left* through gate and follow path to car park

The Birchover and Winster Walks

Millennium Stone, Birchover

Village Cottages

Pond in Birchover

Red Lion Inn

The Lead Miner's Tale

Ay sir, sit th'sen down - no problem at all. Pub's full just now, full all day it is, full every damn day! No one sits at a table on 'is own any more. Make th'sen at 'ome.

Oh Lord no, it's not always like this. Place were a lot quieter till a couple o' weeks back. Never empty, mind. There's always some men just off their shift, or else waitin' to start one. Take it tha's not from round 'ere? Just passin' through? Well, tha's found us at a bad time. Miserable faces everywhere tha looks, must 'ave noticed as much. Just as well we've a decent pub to be sat in - and there's another one down road that'll be just as full. Not many spendin' a lot on the beer, mind. Everyone's missus would be waitin' at 'ome with too much to say. All of us in same damn boat, though, that makes it a bit easier. A man can do a lot o' talkin' over a pint o' warm beer that's been sittin' in front of 'im for well over an hour. All miners, in 'ere, o' course, every damn last one of us. Not th'self, though. Tha's not got the 'ands of a miner!

No doubt tha'll be wonderin' what I'm ramblin' on about. It's the Mill Close - that's where the lot of us work - or did. Not that we're likely to ever get down there again. It's 'ad it, 'as that place, final curtain. Probably just as well there's a war brewin', or so a lot o' folks is sayin'. It'll give a few o' these youngsters some'at to do, at least. Won't do owt for me, an' not for thee neither, I'd say. Did my stint in last one. Bloody 'ard stint it were an' all! Thought we'd put paid to all that nonsense over there.

The Mill Close? Well, tha certainly wouldn't be askin' that, not if tha came from round 'ere, I can tell thee! It's a lead mine. Not that we 'aven't found plenty of other stuff down there over all them years, but lead's the real thing. Biggest producer in England, she is, in fact biggest in 'ole o' Europe. At least there's plenty stocked up to make every bullet they're ever likely to need, if this bloody war starts up. Just like we made most o' the damn bullets for that last war! There's lead mines all over place round 'ere, and there used to be an 'ole lot more - scores of 'em! Does tha know that a couple of 'undred years ago there was more than twenty mines just round Winster? But our Mill Close were the very best of 'em. That were when most o' this village were built, and it 'ad more than twenty inns an 'all! Not quite as good in that way now. But as I said, there's never been a mine what's a patch on Mill Close, nowhere near it! Gone through some bad times, she 'as, but these last few years there's been no lookin' back. Everywhere we turn there's a new vein looms up, and each one's better than one we worked before. There's tons and tons of that stuff still down there - God knows 'ow much - not that we'll ever be getting' it out now. It's there to stay.

What's problem wi' it? 'Ole damn place is flooded, that's what. This man, by name o' Fred, well 'e drills through into a river, or maybe it's a lake, right down in depths o' mine. Not 'is fault, understand, could 'ave been any one of us. Well, wall weakens a bit and now there's 'undreds o' thousands o' gallons an hour coming in, so I'm told. Nowt pumps can do against that, not even our Jumbo - that's what we call biggest one. There's been plenty o' floodin' down there in my lifetime, but never owt like this! Can't see 'em ever getting' it workin' again, not this time. Miracle no one were killed. All got us sen out in time, a lot of us just by skin of us teeth. Thought I were going to join me grand-dad at one point. 'E was drowned down a mine. Not an unusual thing, that, specially in 'is day.

Oh ay, it's always been dangerous work, tha's right there. Men's work - tha'd not get a woman down a mine, not on thy life. Not that anyone'd want 'em! Only places you can get away, down there and in 'ere. It'd be one 'ell of a life if they got everywhere. There's a real good feeling 'mong the men, real pals, never let anyone down. Proper men, they are, not frightened o' a bit of dirt and sweat - proper 'ard men. Not bothered about danger neither, and there's always a good chance of floodin', or else of a roof cavin' in, that's another one. Thing is with a roof, if it do cave in, then tha's not going to be frettin' about it for too long - short and sharp, that's what it'd be! 'Appened to a good pal o' mine, not that long back. Sad thing was, fella 'ad just 'anded 'is notice in an' all. Mind thee, there's not been so many accidents in recent times, not like it were in days past.

Tha what? Oh no, wouldn't want to work anywhere else, to be honest. Probably couldn't do owt else, not now. Not after all them years down there. Went straight back down after last war, and I'd already been down a good few years before it. War came at a good time, as a matter o' fact. Would 'ave been laid off anyway - lead ore were running out just then - or so they all seemed to think. Weren't the case, as it turned out. Place 'as kept me in work ever since, though a good few years back, round 1929, they thought it were running out again. Then this big company - Consolidated Gold Fields of South Africa, it calls itself - puts in a real lot o' money. Bought us biggest electric pumps in the world. That meant we could go a lot deeper. So go deeper we did, and there it were! Richer ore than any we'd ever seen in all our born days. Gold Fields were a good name for it! Lot better than real gold, if th' asks me.

What's them pumps for? Well, they're pumpin' water out o' course, what else? Water 's always been the big problem, it's the problem in all lead mines, but specially in that one. And the deeper we go, the worse it gets. We're usually workin' ankle deep in muddy water, knee deep many a time. And o' course, even in drier bits, it's always slippery underfoot. That's what we all wear clogs for - might seem odd to some folk, but clogs is safest thing. What tha does is, tha takes a pair of old boots to a good cobbler's and 'e'll make 'em into clogs by puttin' on proper wooden soles, wi' nails and clippets. But o' course, all this water, them pumps 'ave to cope with it, get rid of it. They channels it off through long tunnels - soughs, we call 'em . If it weren't for them there's not a lead mine around what could be worked. If pumps can't cope wi' it - say it in a thunderstorm - tha's got to get th'sen up damn quick! But them big pumps can get rid o' thirty million gallons a week. That's 'ow we've managed to get down so low - 'undred and twenty-five fathoms, and deeper. And all that good stuff lies very deep. If tha wants it, tha's to get down for it!

Ay no, it's not lit up, not most of it. Bottoms of shafts is lit, but all rest's dark - that's what we get candles for. Every man gets five candles a shift, and there's about an 'undred and thirty of us on each shift, and there's three shifts a day. That's one 'ell of a lot o' candles! On some levels there's gas about, so if tha needs to go there, tha gets a safety lamp. No one lights a ciggy up round them parts, neither! Course there's a no smokin' rule everywhere in mine, but it's not usually kept to. I've never kept to it m'sen. We can see a boss comin' from way off - can see light from 'is torch - no candles for that lot! Plenty o' time to stub out.

 Tha's got to remember - it's maybe not something tha'll know, not bein' familiar wi' minin' - that a man's not likely to be workin' near a shaft, not near main shaft anyway. That's the one the men get lowered down in, in a cage. I've got nearly two mile to walk once I'm down, to get to where I'll be workin'. Down main shaft, along a level, then I've to climb down another shaft - no cage there to lower me - then walk along again, and so on. Takes a good bit o' time in shift, just to get out there, and then back again. I take snap down wi' me, and some-one'll be brewin' tea. No comin' back up for any meal break - it'd take much too long. Can't come up for lavatory neither! Don't do to be too fussy, down a mine! Once a vein's been found, no one ever knows 'ow far it'll be goin'. A vein goes sideways, like a long pipe, and we follows it as far as it goes, if we can. There's no way of knowin' when it's goin' to peter out.

No, work never stops down there. Goes on all round clock, every day o' week. Three shifts, there are - done 'em all in me time but I like night shift best - quarter to ten at night till quarter to six in mornin'. Wife gives me a decent breakfast, then I'll be in bed around quarter past seven, and I get bed to m'sen 'an all. It suits me and it suits 'er, that does. Very long time since we've wanted owt different. Then I'll be asleep till 'bout two, bit longer if she don't set about wakin' me up by clatterin' around. Like to do a bit of gardenin' in afternoons. It's only a patch, but it's alright for a few carrots and cabbages. Get dinner about five, if she 'asn't spent all afternoon gossipin'. Beats me what women find to natter about. It's about nowt, usually, but that never seems to stop 'em!

No, it's not too bad a life. That mine 'as looked after Winster well enough, and a few other villages too. When tha thinks of all them folk what's been laid off in towns, or 'avin' to take wage cuts! Won war, didn't we and then what do a lot o' folk get for it? No money, no jobs, no nothin'. And now it looks as if the 'ole bloody mess is goin' to start again! The laugh is, some German company's just offered to drain this mine for us, so I've 'eard. Claim they've got better stuff to do it than we 'ave. But that Goldfields lot - and they've got all the say-so now - they've told 'em no thanks, and in no uncertain terms. Too many nasty things goin' on over there. They don't want owt to do with 'em. Whether our lot'll manage to drain place out is another thing. Doubt it very much, mesen. And that's nearly eight 'undred men out, what with smelter as well. 'Cos smelter's no damn good to anyone, not without mine.

Four 'undred years, that's 'ow long Mill Close 'as been goin'. It's the only reason why Winster exists! That mine's brought this place some real riches over the years - tha's only got to look at some of them fancy buildings in the 'igh street, and then all them cottages up on this 'ill. And now it all looks as if the 'ole damn lot's at an end.

Well cheers sir, I will an' all! Throat's gone dry, what with all this talkin' - 'ope I've not bored thee to death. It's not often we see a new face at Miners Standard. Ay, another pint'd go down a real treat!

Historical note:

In 1938 miners in the Mill Close hit an underground lake or river, and it took months to
pump the mine clear. It finally closed in 1940, with over 2,000 litres a minute still pouring in.

Lead miners were renowned for being heavy beer drinkers. They believed beer helped
protect them from lead poisoning. The Odin mine was near Castleton, one of hundreds of
lead mines in the Peak District.

'Come fellows drink
- drink, drink your fill,

Full soon we must
gang up the hill

Where Odin rich
in shining ore

Shall give us glasses
- hundreds more;

Then luck to Odin
- golden mine,

With metal bright,
like the sun doth shine.'

THIS CARVING IS AN EXACT REPLICA OF
"T' OWD MAN OF BONSALL".
THE ORIGINAL EARLY MEDIEVAL CARVING, THE EARLIEST
REPRESENTATION OF A DERBYSHIRE LEAD MINER,
STOOD FOR CENTURIES IN BONSALL PARISH CHURCH.
DURING THE RESTORATION WORK IN 1863 IT WAS
REMOVED FOR SAFEKEEPING.
EVENTUALLY IT WAS MOVED TO WIRKSWORTH PARISH
CHURCH WHERE IT IS BUILT INTO THE SOUTH TRANSEPT.
THIS REPLICA WAS CARVED BY
GRAHAM BARFIELD OF BOLE HILL
IN DECEMBER 2002

Walk 7

DARLEY BRIDGE
B5057
CAMBRIDGE WOOD
RED LION
WENSLEY
TEARSALL FARM
CLOUGH WOOD
LIMESTONE WAY
SLALEY LOW FARM
BONSALL LANE
B5057
O.P.
CAR PARK
SCHOOL
THE MARKET HOUSE (NAT. TRUST)
OLD BOWLING GREEN
WINSTER
W.C.
N
R.P.
Winster
Wensley

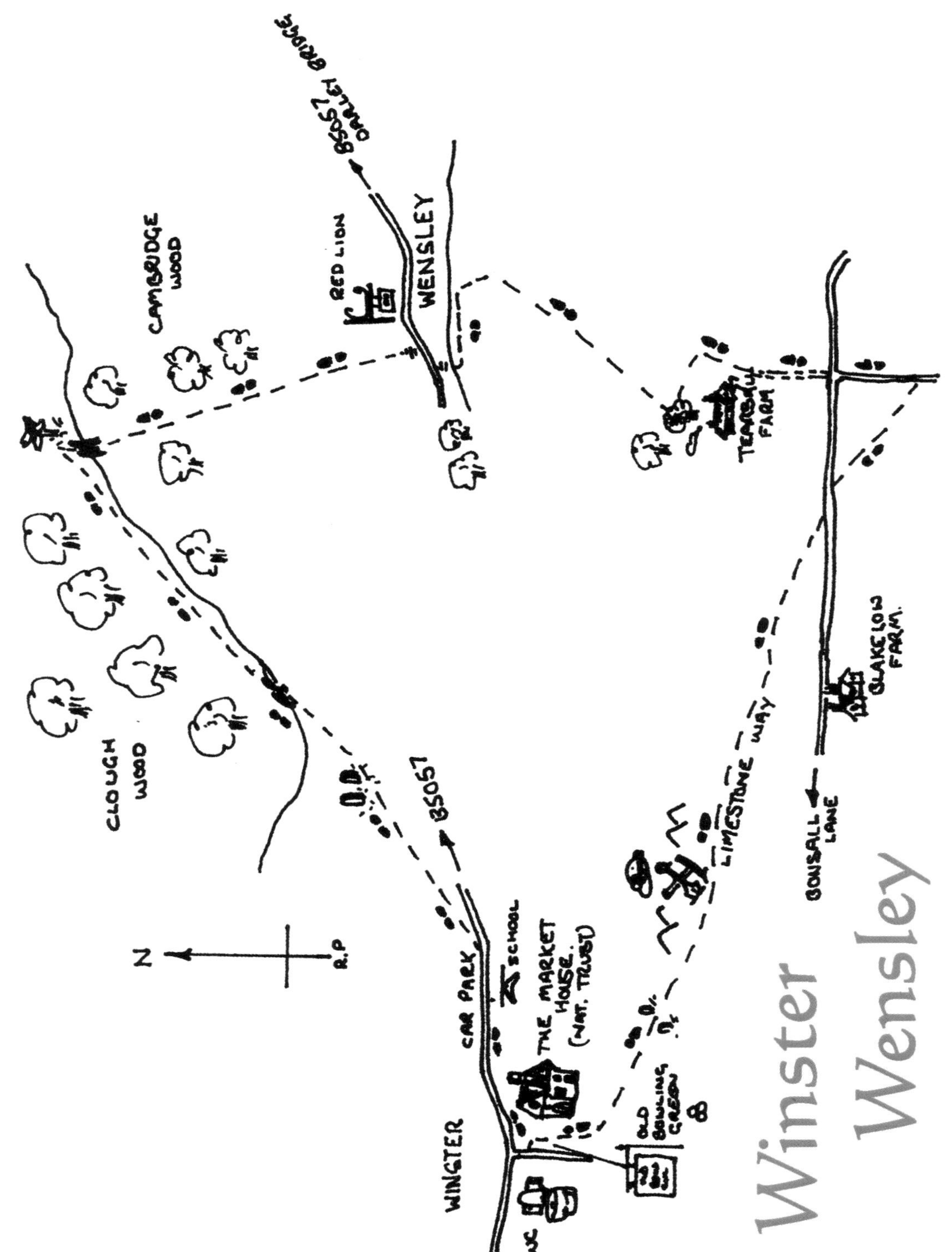

Walk 7

Winster - Limestone Way - Wensley

About this walk

A really beautiful walk with some stunning views. It starts in the attractive and historic village of Winster which is worth an amble round, including a quick look inside Market House. The route offers a variety of fields, hills, valleys and woodlands.

Distance	8km 5 miles
Terrain	A moderate walk with a few steady climbs and one fairly steep and uneven descent through Cambridge Wood. At the end of the route there is a very short distance on a country road with no pavement. Some areas can be very muddy after rain but the surface is mainly good underfoot.
Map	OS Explorer OL24 The Peak District, White Peak area. 1:25 000 scale.
Starting Point	Parking in free car park next to Winster Primary School on the B5057, just before you enter the village from the direction of Wensley. Public toilets just after start of walk. (see instruction 3). Grid reference SK 245 606 .
Refreshments	Winster has a village store and a Post Office. The Old Bowling Green pub is near the start of the walk, The Miners Standard Inn is a short drive from the centre of the village, up the hill. Both serve food.

✓ **Before leaving car park, note information board near entrance.**

1. From car park entrance, turn *left* and follow pavement past school and through village

2. At **Market House** (old National Trust building across left-hand pavement) walk along left-hand side of building

✓ **Winster is one of the oldest villages in the Peak and was once the centre of the local lead mining industry. In the 18th century, it was thriving and prosperous with a larger population than today. It still has some fine buildings from that era, especially Winster Hall, half-way along the main street, and the Dower House, in front of the church. The Market House was constructed in the 16th and 17th centuries. It was the first property in this area to be acquired by the National Trust.**

3. Turn *left* up road and *left* again just past **The Old Bowling Green** pub (there are public toilets a few steps further up here)

4. A few paces beyond toilet, just in front of house, turn *right* through stile by gateway

5. Head up right-hand side of field (this is the right of way). Turn *left* where paths meet and go through gap in wall. (If field is crossed diagonally, you come to gap directly)

✓ **Look back for a good view of village and surrounding area.**

6. Bear diagonally right uphill to wall opposite and go through gap in wall (by trees)

7. Continue as path bears away from wall on left-hand side. Follow path as it bears up to wall opposite

Market House, Winster

8. Go through gap in wall and continue across top of field (low wall on right)

✓ **Many of the lumps and bumps in the ground are the remains of lead mining activities. These are visible around many villages of the Peak, where workings dramatically changed the landscape. Many old miners' paths are now public footpaths. Disused shafts were largely uncapped until fairly recently. Over the centuries, many lives were lost in these death traps.**

9. Go over stile in opposite wall and continue across field to wall opposite (passing 2 stone posts)

10. Go through gated stile in wall and continue along path, as it bears slightly right towards top right-hand corner of wall opposite

11. Go through further gated stile and continue (wall on right). <u>A little further up</u>, cross stile on right, turn *left* and continue on (wall now on left)

12. Pass through stile in broken down wall and continue on up (keeping wall on left)

13. Go through gap in wall and in a while through further wall (broken down)

14. Bear diagonally right up field towards stile in middle of right-hand wall

15. Pass through stile, bear left and through next stile in left-hand wall close by

16. Continue slightly diagonally across a further 2 fields (with gap in wall and 1 stile)

17. From stile, cross track (which leads to **Blakelow Farm** on right) and continue straight on across field

18. Cross further stile and bear diagonally right, through middle of field to corner

19. Cross stile and turn *left* up road

20. Very shortly, go through stile on right and bear diagonally left to top left-hand corner of field

21. Walk through gap in wall and bear left to stile in left-hand wall close by

22. Go through stile in broken down wall, follow path around mound and across to opposite wall

23. Pass through further broken down wall and bear right towards gap (approximately $^2/_3$ along right-hand wall)

24. Walk through gap in wall and cross field diagonally left to stile near left-hand corner

25. Go over stile, turn *left* and immediately *left* again down lane

26. Pass ruined farm building on right and follow lane down to road

27. Cross road and go straight on through left-hand gateway and down track

28. At bottom of track, turn *right* (away from **Tersall Farm**)

29. Go through gateway and follow track up and round

30. Continue to follow track round as it turns left by quarry

✓ **Good view of Matlock Town to your right.**

31. At end of track, go over stile by gateway (ignore gate ahead) and bear right

32. After a few paces, head down to bottom left-hand corner of field

33. Go through gap in wall and head slightly right towards ruined building. Cross stile on left of building and head down hill, keeping close to wall on left

✓ **Riber Castle lies on the right in the distance. The castle was built by John Smedley, a wealthy mill owner, who made Matlock famous for hydrotherapy treatments in the late 19th century. It is presently in ruins, but there are plans to redevelop it.**

34. Near bottom of field, cross stile on left and follow path (wall on both sides)

35. At end of path, turn *right* and walk down hill (wall on right)

36. As this path ends, with gateway on right, turn *left* and follow path down towards village of **Wensley**

37. At bottom of slope, turn *left* and go up track, past cottages on right

38. Follow round to small gate on right, then take path along and up steps to road

39. Turn *right* and at first cottage cross road, go up steps and through gateway

40. Head up right-hand side of field (ignore gateway), eventually passing underground water reservoir near top

41. Go over top of hill and follow path down, keeping to right-hand side

42. At bottom right-hand corner, cross stile, head down steps and through wooded area

43. Pass small pond on right and continue on down

44. At bottom of hill, go over footbridge, take a few paces up onto track and turn *right*

45. Shortly, as track meets another, turn *left*. Then after a few paces, turn *left* again and follow path along (ignore paths going down to left)

46. Continue on (stream on left), cross small tributary stream and continue along path for some distance

47. At end of path, leaving wooded area, cross small footbridge and stile

48. With your back to this stile, head up hill and slightly to the right (next stile is up beyond 2 stone posts)

49. Cross this stile and bear right up hill, through further stile, then continue up and round

50. Go through next stile and follow path as it bears slightly left, up to opposite wall

51. Go over stile and bear left, up to left-hand wall by road

52. Go through stile, turn *right* and follow road to car park (on opposite side of road)

Winster Village

Walk 8

Birchover
Stanton Moor
Nine Ladies

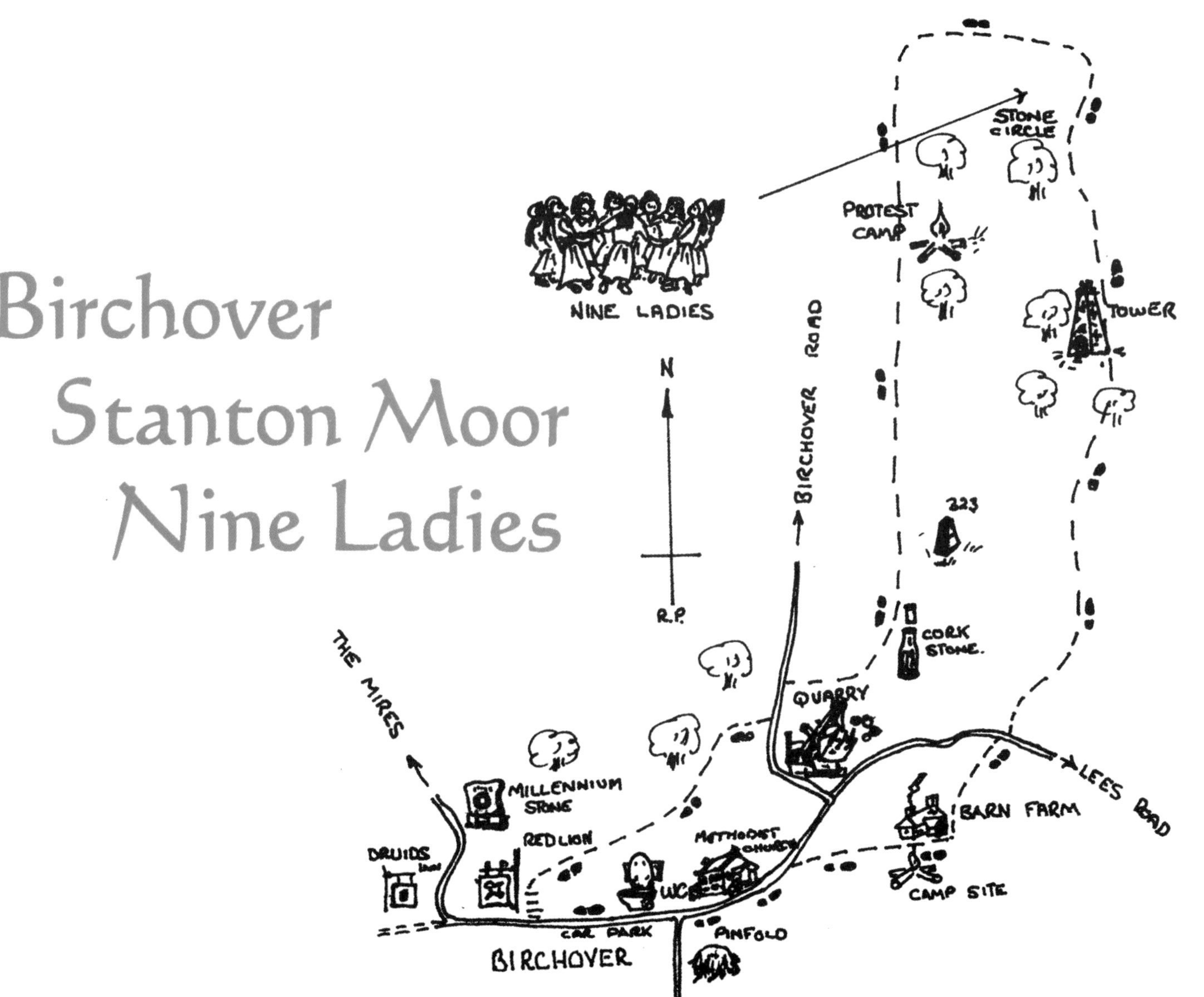

Walk 8

Birchover - Stanton Moor - Nine Ladies (stone circle)

About this walk

This is a delightful but unchallenging walk, with attractive views from the edges. It offers a wide variety of landscape with some archaeological and historical interest.

Distance	4.8km 3 miles
Terrain	A fairly easy walk with only gentle inclines and reasonably even underfoot. It includes pathways, moorland, rural roads and woodlands. One short descent, near the end of the walk, does require a little care.
Map	OS Explorer OL24 The Peak District, White Peak area. 1:25 000 scale.
Starting Point	There is usually ample on-road parking available on the High Street in Birchover village. The general store and public toilets are also here. Grid reference SK 238 621.
Refreshments	Birchover has two attractive inns, the Red Lion and Druid Inn. There is also a village store selling a wide range of goods.

1. From public toilets on **Birchover High Street**, walk up road, past shop and **Wesleyan Reform Church** building on left (ignore path on right just after church)

2. Shortly, at entrance to **Barn Farm**, turn *right* and follow driveway straight up (keeping farmhouse on left)

3. Go through stile in wall, turn *left* and immediately go through further stile by gateway and along track, past back of farm

4. Follow buildings round into yard and through wide gateway, slightly to right

5. Take track bearing right and up (wall on right) and on meeting road, go through stile and turn *right* along road

6. Very shortly after, cross road to go over stile on left, and follow main path up to **Stanton Moor**

7. As path divides, take right-hand path

8. At large rock on right, cross stile and turn *left*

✓ **All along this edge, there are attractive views and it is worth going occasionally to the vantage points to fully appreciate these. The lead smelting company, Enthoven, is also clearly visible.**

9. Eventually, as path forms T-junction (rock to right with good view!) turn *left* and follow path, keeping tower on left

✓ **This wooded area is under threat of renewed quarrying. Since 1999 a protest camp of 'Eco-Warriors' has occupied land around the Nine Ladies circle. This camp still exists at the time of writing.**

10. After a few minutes, take stile on left and follow path

11. Walk through stone circle and straight on past single stone

✓ **This circle, known as the 'Nine Ladies' is said in folklore to have been formed by women being turned to stone for dancing on the Sabbath. The 'King Stone', just a few yards away, was said to have been their fiddler. The area around the circle has a serene atmosphere and can be a peaceful place to sit and contemplate.**

12. Keep on as path bears right and at pathways junction (old quarry to right) turn *left* along path

13. Keep to main path and where paths meet, take first *left*

14. Continue along path (remnants of old quarries on right) and continue as path winds across moor, passing trig point on left

✓ **Trig points were a tool for surveying in the days before electronic positioning aids were available (GPS etc). Typically, a trig point is a concrete post set on a high point such as a hill, with a metal disc inset in the top, where a measuring instrument could be placed.**

15. As path meets another one, by large rock (with climbing rings), turn *right*

✓ **This stone is known as Cork Stone, and it's hard to imagine it has been shaped by the elements and not sculptured by man. It has footholds chiselled into the soft rock and metal hand holds to enable the adventurous to stand on the top and enjoy the view.**

16. Go over stile, down to road and turn *left*. Continue to follow road towards **Birchover**

17. Just past stone company on left, turn *right* through wide gateway, go straight through car park and onto path

✓ **You can now see Youlgrave village in the distance ahead.**

18. Keep to path as it bears left and down through wooded area

19. As wall ends, turn *left* down steps to village

20. On reaching road (**Red Lion** on right, **Druid Inn** a little further down on right) turn *left* up pavement to return to car

Cork Stone

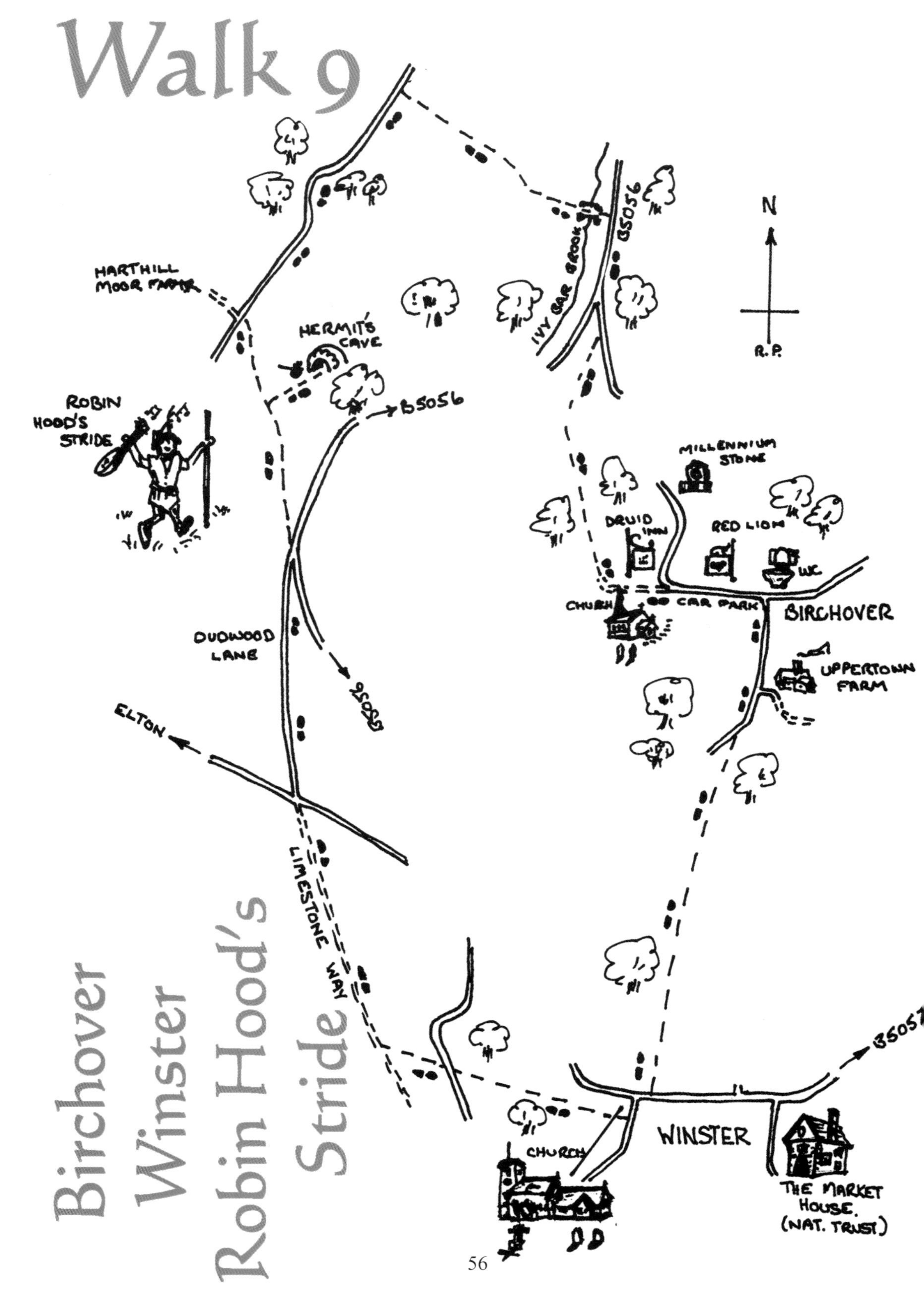

Walk 9
Birchover
Winster
Robin Hood's Stride
N
R.P.
HARTHILL MOOR FARM
HERMIT'S CAVE
ROBIN HOOD'S STRIDE
B5056
IVY BAR BROOK
B5056
DUDWOOD LANE
B5056
ELTON
LIMESTONE WAY
MILLENNIUM STONE
DRUID INN
RED LION
WC
CHURCH
CAR PARK
BIRCHOVER
UPPERTOWN FARM
B5057
CHURCH
WINSTER
THE MARKET HOUSE.
(NAT. TRUST)

Walk 9
Birchover - Winster - Robin Hood's Stride

About this walk

This walk offers a fascinating background of history and legend. It has striking views and you can absorb the rich variation in landscape and village. On this walk it is worth taking the short optional visits up to the Hermit's cave and into Winster to the Market Hall. There are plenty of good spots to stop for a break or a picnic along the way.

Distance   8.5km   5.3 miles

Terrain   This is a moderate walk with a few gradual hills. Mainly sound underfoot with a variety of surfaces, including fields, lanes, pavements and footpaths. Towards the end of the walk there is one short stretch of roadway with no pavement and care needs to be taken.

Map   OS Explorer OL24 The Peak District, White Peak area. 1:25 000 scale.

Starting Point   There is usually ample on-road parking available on the High Street in Birchover village. The general store and public toilets are also here. Grid reference SK 238 621.

Refreshments   Birchover has two attractive inns, the Red Lion and Druid Inn. There is also a village store selling a wide range of goods. Winster has The Old Bowling Green Inn, the Miners Standard Inn, a Post Office and a general store.

1. From public toilets on **Birchover Main Street**, walk up road, past shop and turn *right* down **Uppertown Lane**

2. Continue down lane. As lane rises and then forks, carry straight on past **Uppertown Farm**

✓ **Notice the stocks at side of farm.**

3. Follow lane down, ignoring paths to left and right

4. As lane bears right, go through gate and stile on left and bear slightly right across field, to bottom of boundary (in direction of village of **Winster** on hillside)

5. Go through gap in boundary and then slightly diagonally right to opposite boundary

6. Go through small gate, down incline and straight across, then through small gate and stile and straight up

7. Pass through narrow stile and continue up to opposite bank. Go over stile and head down field, keeping to right-hand side

8. Join narrow paved path (low wall on right), follow steps up and continue (ignore path joining from left)

9. As path splits, go through stile and gate on left (ignore stile in wall on right). Carry straight on up field towards farm buildings (ignore path to left)

10. Go through small gate beside large gate and barn. Continue through farmyard (keep to wall on right) and through gateway (or gap beside it)

11. Carry straight on, across private driveway (**The Byre**) and through small stile opposite

12. Walk along path (wall and houses both sides) to main road

✓ Winster is one of the oldest villages in the Peak and was once the centre of the local lead mining industry. In the 18th century it was thriving and prosperous with a larger population than today. It has some fine buildings from that era. Chief of these is Winster Hall, which stands half-way along the main street, and the Dower House, which is in front of the church. The Market House was constructed in the 16th and 17th centuries. It was the first property in this area to be acquired by the National Trust. Winster still has the feel of a lead-mining centre, with rows of former miners' cottages.

❖ Turn left if you wish to visit Winster and rejoin the walk at point 13.

13. Cross road, turn *right* and after a few paces turn *left*. Cross road and walk up **West Bank**

14. After a few steps, turn *right* and very shortly go through iron gate or stile

15. Carry straight on through cemetery (ignore path bearing right to church of **St. John the Baptist**)

16. Shortly, go through stile and follow path as it bears up left (keep attractive large stone house on your right)

17. Keep straight on, go through wooden stile and a further stile with gate, leading out of small copse

18. Go straight across field, through derelict wall to gate and stile in wall opposite

19. Go over this stile, turn *right* and after a few paces cross road and go over stile opposite

20. Bear right and go through stile in wall just ahead. Go straight across field and through further stile, by gateway in wall opposite

21. Follow path (keeping to right-hand wall). Go through further stile (by derelict building)

22. Go straight on and through stile in opposite wall. Then bear right to far right-hand corner of field

23. Go through stile, turn *right* and cross lane. Continue along track

✓ **As you walk along, note good view of Birchover village across on the right.**

24. Eventually, as track meets road, turn *left*, then immediately *right*, into **Dudwood Lane**

25. Continue down lane (ignore all paths off). Eventually, as lane curves right to meet road (**Dudwood Farm** entrance on left), go straight on through small gate by large one. Head on up track (large rock face ahead)

26. Pass through stone posted gateway, bear left and follow path up left-hand side of field

27. Almost at top of field, ignore stile in wall on right by **Hilary's Seat**. Go through stile by gateway and continue up track

❖ **If you wish to visit the Hermit's Cave, go over steps in wall on right, opposite Robin Hood's Stride and follow path to Hermit's Cave (if open, easier access through gateway a little further on). Afterwards continue from point 28.**

✓ **The Hermit's Cave at Cratcliff Rocks was at one time home to a hermit. Under an overhang of rock a carved crucifix remains. In the Middle Ages, hermits were looked on as holy men. Appointed to lonely places by a bishop, they rendered hospitality and assistance to travellers.**

28. Continue up track and shortly go over stile on left, by 2 large gateways. Then continue straight on (wall on right)

✓ **The gritstone rocks are called Robin Hood's Stride. Legend has it that Robin strode between the tower-like stones at either end of the tor. An alternative local name is 'Mock Beggar's Hall'.**

29. Very shortly, go over stile on right, by gateway in wall. Then bear diagonally left to top corner of field

✓ **Look out for the Bronze Age Stone Circle in distance on right. This is known as 'Nine Stone Close' (though in fact only four are visible) or the Grey Ladies. Legend has it that on moonlit nights the ladies begin to dance. In Midsummer the stones appear to be aligned with the two peaks of Robin Hood's Stride.**

30. Go over stile in wall, by gateway. Then bear diagonally left across field and cross further stile, close to corner

31. Turn *right* along lane (by entrance to **Harthill Moor Farm**) and continue as lane curves down, ignoring paths off

Dower House, Winster

32. A few minutes after reaching bottom of hill, just before lane curves left, look out for gates opposite each other

✓ **Note village of Youlgrave in distance on left.**

33. Go through small gate on right, just after large one. Head straight across field

34. Go through gate opposite and down path (heading towards road in distance)

35. Cross small gated bridge, bear right and up to gate by road

36. After gate, turn *right* (verge here can be narrow so care needs to be taken)

37. After approximately 5 minutes, turn *left* along road to **Birchover**

38. Shortly after road bends, turn *right* to cross grassy bridge over stream

39. Go over stile, then follow path as it bears left. At top of bank, go straight on up across field to top corner

40. Go through gateway, turn *left* and head up field to wooded hillock (wall on left)

41. At top of field, in front of hillock, go through gate and turn *left* along track

42. Almost immediately, go down left-hand of 2 tracks

43. Continue along track as it leads past the **Old Vicarage** and **Wesleyan Chapel** and up into **Birchover**. As lane meets road (**Druid Inn** on left) turn *right* to return to car

✓ **Note the Birchover Millennium stone, opposite the Druid Inn. Mark Eaton carved the stone, which was donated by the local quarry. It weighs nearly a ton and a half.**

The Youlgrave Walks

Lomberdale Hall, Middleton

Monyash Village

Old Chapel in Middleton

Monyash Village Cross

The Lover's Tale

Sometimes I stand a while beside his grave - an unusual monument altogether, though simple enough, not showy. Thomas Bateman, renowned archaeologist and antiquarian, beloved by his family and held in deep affection by his friends. A man who knew his vocation, who sensed what should be done with his life. And one day, the most important thing he needed to do was to be well rid of me.

A sudden event, that was. Perhaps I'd always had a fear of it, but never truly allowed myself to expect it. Desperately happy, we always were, in each other's company. Thomas passionate and intense in his hunger for me, and I certainly no less so in my need for him. But there was more than lust between us. He had willingly confronted both public condemnation and his grandfather's anger in order to be with me, laughing scornfully at such reactions, as often as not. We were young. We were free beings, Thomas and myself, or so both of us believed - unrestrained, casting aside a stuffy convention, indifferent to the narrow, stunted opinions of others.

But not indifferent to the stark terms of a will. A will carefully worded by his grandfather, the man after whom my Thomas had been named. The old man died in the May of 1874, at the good age of eighty-seven. My own Thomas was just twenty-five. The funeral respectfully conducted, I witnessed him listen attentively as the conditions of inheritance were read to him - and with his own father long dead that inheritance concerned Thomas alone. A change appeared in the eyes of the man who loved me, a subtle, distant change but one which instantly sealed my fate.

The words were more direct, more personal, than you might expect a legal document to express. Thomas was to end his 'criminal connection' with me. If he did not, his benefit in the estate 'shall absolutely cease and be void'. And there was to be little time of grace, the will set an absolute deadline of three months. Thus, by 26th August 1847, I was to be removed entirely from his life. And the recompense? It was total ownership of the Middleton Estate. This, of course, included Middleton Hall, the Georgian mansion built by his grandfather. It encompassed Lomberdale Hall - our own home - and land of around three thousand acres. Not least, it would bring to him the almost feudal service and respect of the villagers. People for whom we had long been a subject of malicious gossip.

You may already be hardening against Thomas in your heart. Perhaps unjustly. Who would not do the same? Would I, in that position, have not done the same? He could not marry me. The problem was not one of class, though in this matter I stood well below him. I was a married woman already - wife of Mr. Mason, a boatman on Cromford Canal.

Perhaps I should take you back a little further, even into Thomas's life before the time I entered it. Thomas's mother, Mary (a name I share), died when he was a mere nine months old and she herself only twenty-two years. His father, William, was grief-stricken and moved with his baby son from their home in Rowsley, to live with his own father at Middleton Hall. More than ample room, of course, though a sad lack of female influence.

Perhaps the three got on well enough together - Thomas always said they did. Indeed, the older Thomas is quoted as describing his little grandson as "one of the finest children ever born." William was lucky, despite the tragic loss of his wife. He shared a fine home, had no worries for money, he could choose his activities. Earlier in his youth he had developed an interest in antiquity, encouraged by the huge library at Middleton Hall. From this came the thrill of digging up several of the area's mysterious barrows - ancient burial grounds of our forgotten ancestors - forcing them to yield their secrets to the fork, the spade, the pick. My Thomas accompanied him from a very early age, the quiet father and the far more assertive son uniting in this love of earthy exploration.

But William was not strong. Years of failing health - I don't think Thomas ever truly knew the cause - brought on his death at the age of forty-eight. Now there remained only grandfather and grandson, two men of the name Thomas, aged seventy-five and thirteen, both of them very determined characters. The younger man retained his interest in the digging, in unearthing our primitive pagan past. On holiday from the boarding school in Liverpool to which he was sent, he roamed the woods and moors with a companion, William, while at the same time devouring, as his father did before him, the works in his grandfather's library. Thomas and William became inseparable, though Thomas had an intellect far beyond that of his friend. Digging up the fascinating pieces from beneath the burial mounds could never have been enough. They must be examined, measured, documented, understood. Theories must be proposed to explain them. This was a rich science, and it began to carry his name far beyond the boundaries of the place he lived.

But I must enter here. A few years later, Thomas's eyes chanced upon me, and our physical delight in each other took hold with suddenness and consumed us both in its thrall. I doubt at first he asked himself if I might be already married. It was some time before I told him, because in truth it barely seemed to matter. I was young, without a child, my husband an easily content man without insight or suspicion. He made little fuss when Thomas, after receiving a part of his father's money at his coming of age, obtained a small house for the two of us in Bakewell. As our life together became known, the only wrath expressed was that of the older Thomas, enraged and humiliated. But my Thomas remained defiant, confident of his grandfather's deep sentiment for him. They had already known many differences of opinion - fiercely expressed - but never had his financial means been cut off and nor were they now. Deaf to the pious voices around us, he lay entirely under my spell.

I am sure others believed it would end within a few months at most - just as long as it took for a young man's passion to be fully satisfied and to start its ebb. We defied them. Many months later, we moved from Matlock Street, Bakewell, to Thomas's newly-built house in Middleton, Lomberdale Hall. Here we were to live for three more years. For quite some time, my sister joined us there, a generosity that seemed to fire the local gossips even more.

In the September of 1844 - to my great delight - we travelled together to Canterbury for the first great Congress of the newly formed British Archaeological Association. Outside the narrow confines of Middleton, of course, we were presumed to be man and wife. The following year, we toured in leisurely style around the North, partly for Thomas to visit the huge excavations then taking place around York. Again, not an eyebrow was raised.

Why could it not continue? Of course it could not. Had there been a child, perhaps that might have saved me, but I was not fertile, a fact for which Thomas was no doubt grateful.

There was no time for him to lose. He had to tell me his decision, but of course I knew of it already. I shed not a tear in his presence, I am proud enough in nature, if not in birth. Within two days I chose to leave, though not penniless - he was an honourable man. Since that moment I have not set my eyes closely upon him, not once. But I have never lived far away, and I have known much of his doings. Especially in the weeks that followed.

Thomas decided to marry quickly. Marriage was not a condition of the will, but perhaps he sensed that respectability must be promptly restored. There existed no one else he loved - quite obviously not - but there was at Lomberdale a young housekeeper, twenty-two years old. Not a beautiful woman, and little higher in status than me. The sister of his barrow digging friend, William Parker. Sarah must have been shocked indeed to receive his offer, but I doubt she hesitated long. Advantages can be quickly weighed up. On 2nd August the two were married at Bakewell register office, and a few days later he was formally handed the keys to Middleton Hall and its beautiful estate. On that occasion, the happy pair were driven in their carriage through the village, where there was feasting and celebration, free ale at the Bateman Arms, and a huge bonfire as the evening drew on. Thomas was now truly the country squire, a man of substance. The following year, unsurprisingly, Sarah gave birth to his first child.

I do not seek to sound bitter. Without such conformity, such observance of the rules, he may never have achieved what he later did. We did not live in a world of choice. A sense of freedom during youth was little more than acting out a fantasy. And he did achieve, did Mr. Thomas Bateman, aided by an undemanding wife who supported him quietly and unquestioningly, who laid no claim to any ambition or wants of her own. His energies were freed and both the excavations and studies grew apace.

Thomas revealed the secrets of not scores, but hundreds of prehistoric burial grounds - on a scale no longer possible and with a freedom that would no doubt be the envy of any archaeologist of a later time. There were no rules, no restrictions, no hard won permission to be sought, no hand of authority involved. But Thomas was not a common grave robber. 'Barrow digger' was not a term of abuse used against him, though of course his methods and tools could only be those of the time. No doubt to your own age his ways would seem crude, even greedy. He was, however, meticulous. The skulls, the bones, the urns and the ornaments he found were carefully preserved in the rapidly growing collection at Lomberdale Hall. Each one he painstakingly examined, against the background of his vast reading and knowledge. They were minutely documented in his papers. And not only did he engage in the digging himself, along with his group of trusted companions, but Thomas organised many other excavations in Yorkshire and Staffordshire. Middleton came to be seen, so I read, as a pioneering centre within English archaeology. Our lovely Lomberdale Hall was almost doubled in size to house his work. Alongside, of course, the growing number of his children.

Thomas was fortunate. Wealth means freedom to pursue the activities you choose, profitable or not. In justice to him, he seemed a much liked man, even in his guise as arch

Tory landowner (such very different views from his Liberal father). He had a little school built for village children, though other than this little changed in Middleton. Occasionally villagers have been invited to eat, drink and make merry at his expense. I am acquainted with people who attended such a party, as the Crimean War finally drew to its close. At least three hundred villagers took tea in the gardens and a very great quantity of ale was drunk.

I think it was in the autumn of 1850 that I heard Thomas was very ill, indeed that he was expected to die. He did not die, perhaps helped by the hasty arrival of an eminent specialist from London. I am not aware of what the illness was, but recovery from it seemed to make Thomas for more religious than before. I heard he was seeking to atone for the sins of his past, a suggestion that caused me no little pain, even after so very many years. Thereafter, he became a strict non-conformist, in the steps of his grandfather. A faithful pillar of that institution, in both prayer and financial generosity.

In August 1861, Thomas died. There had been a sudden illness - again I am ignorant as to its cause. I understand his life ended in a serious haemorrhage, very early on a dull and wet morning. He was thirty-nine, and had achieved much, but it is cruelly young for such an intellect to be destroyed.

I often wonder if he was happy. There must have been satisfaction in his work, and perhaps that was what truly mattered to him. Sarah gave birth to five children, but to only one son, named Thomas William. From the day I left, I sense a great dullness settled itself over his life, an indifferent acceptance of social requirements. Perhaps I am mistaken, I am hardly unbiased.

Sarah died just a year ago, and only five years after Thomas. The good age reached by his grandfather was certainly not enjoyed by those who followed. She is now buried here also, a fact which kept me away for a time, but now it seems of less matter. Young children were left without their parents - the youngest, Clara Theodora, was but three years old. I believe Sarah's younger sister lived at Lomberdale for some time (just as mine did). Perhaps she now shoulders some of the care. Their son, Thomas William, must be about fifteen now. Like my Thomas, he finds himself alone at a sadly young age. I hear he is not a boy of his father's character and that he is querulous with his four sisters. It seems he has no interest whatever in the past, but indeed is showing little sense of any future path of his own. I feel a sympathy for the lad, even a desire to see him, to talk with him, though that is almost certain never to occur. I am sure my name has long been blotted out from every memory and certainly from all mention. I am the woman who never was.

If you are strolling through Middleton, take the overgrown path that leads along to Thomas's grave. You will hardly be impressed - it is plain and rather neglected. Perhaps someone will one day give of their time to make the place a little more welcoming. The grave lies on a pleasant hill, close to his home, and seems known to but few. Thomas set out in his life to reveal the secrets of the dead, the dead of a forgotten world, and this task he fulfilled. Few men are fortunate enough to know such fulfilment. Perhaps there should be no sadness for his life, not even inside my own heart.

Walk 10

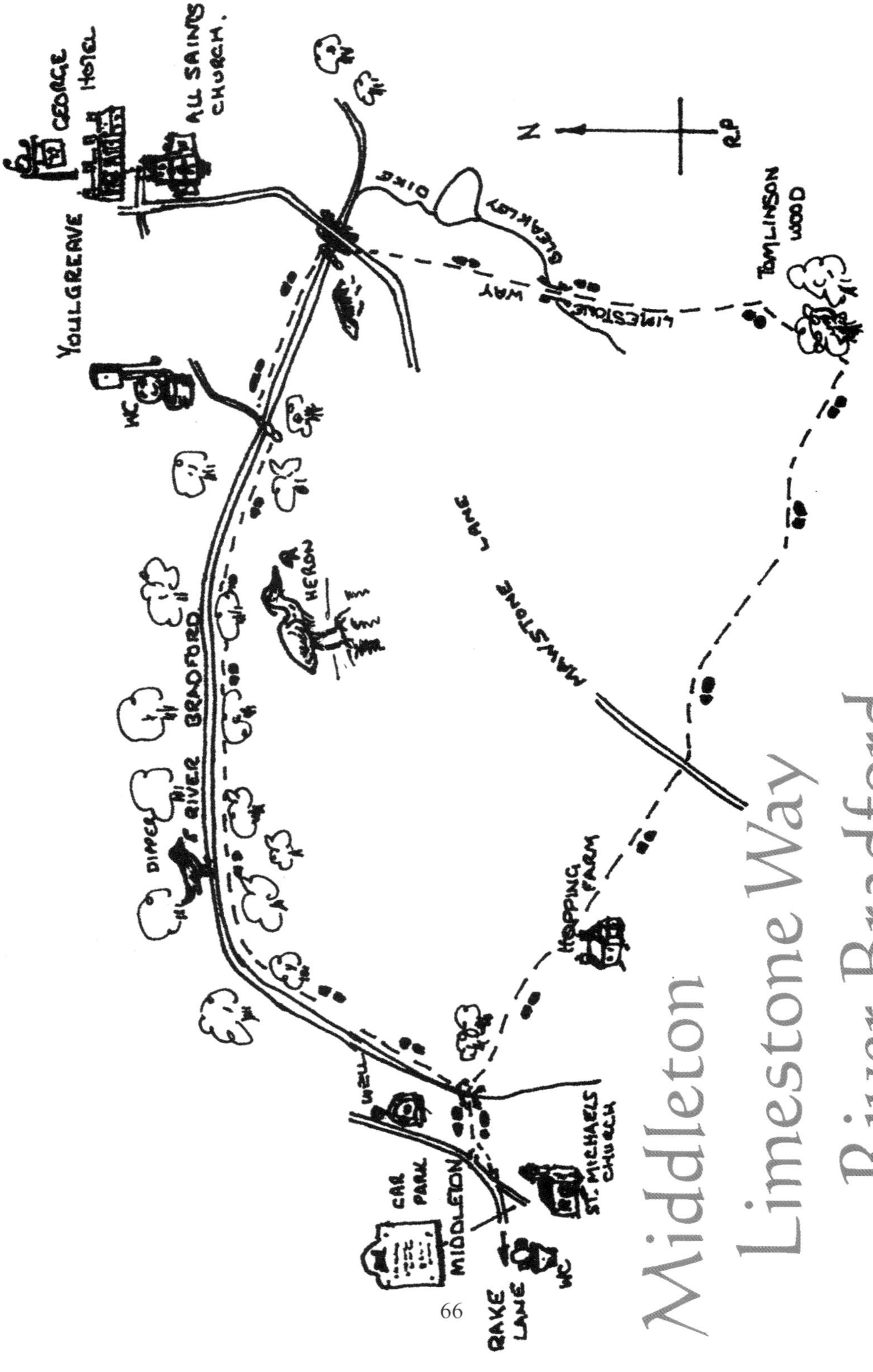

Middleton

Limestone Way

River Bradford

GEORGE HOTEL

ALL SAINTS CHURCH.

YOULGREAVE

WC

DIKE

N R.D

BLEAKLEY

LIMESTONE WAY

TOMLINSON WOOD

RIVER BRADFORD

HERON

MAWSTONE LANE

DIPPER

HOPPING FARM

STEPS

CAR PARK

MIDDLETON

ST. MICHAELS CHURCH

WC

RAKE LANE

Walk 10

Middleton - Limestone Way - River Bradford

About this walk

A truly lovely walk, in a dale that deserves greater acclaim. An often underappreciated area that offers a tranquil setting as you amble along the bank of the River Bradford. This natural and unspoilt dale is one of our favoured routes.

Distance	7km 4.3 miles
Terrain	A moderate route, with only one longish but steady rise, near the start. Mostly level or downhill after this section. A mixture of fields, hillside, tracks, pavement and riverside. May be muddy in a few places.
Map	OS Explorer OL24 The Peak District, White Peak area. 1:25 000 scale.
Starting Point	Middleton (by Youlgrave) village 'square'. There is usually ample on-road parking available in Middleton. There are public toilets by the War Memorial Gardens on the 'square'. Grid Reference SK 195 631.
Refreshments	Café in Bradford Dale with limited summer opening hours.

1. From **Middleton** village 'square', facing war memorial garden and playground, take road to garden's left and then almost immediately turn *left* again

2. Carry on as this road shortly becomes a track, and a few metres further down, bear right and go over stile.

3. Continue up (keeping wall on left) and shortly walk along side of small wood

4. At end of wood, cross stile and continue down (wall and stream to left)

5. As wall and fence end on left, head down and cross small footbridge over stream. Turn *right* and walk along path

6. After short time, as main path heads to wall at top of field, bear right to right-hand wall

7. Cross stile and go straight on up. Cross stile in next wall (farm buildings in sight ahead)

8. Go straight across to farmhouse, through gated stile and on past farm (caravan park ahead)

9. Go through stone stile, straight across track and through next stile in wall

10. Follow path up field (wall on left). At top of field, go through stile in left-hand corner

11. Follow path to left, through next stile, then turn *right* and follow path up hill (wall on right)

12. Go through gate, across lane, through gate opposite and continue up

❖ **View of Youlgrave village over to left.**

13. On approaching broken down wall, bear left and cross stile in that wall

14. Continue up and cross stile in top wall, then go straight across field to opposite wall

15. Pass through stile and continue straight on

16. Cross track and then go over stile (a little to the right of gateway)

17. Continue straight on, go through gateway, then bear slightly right towards opposite wall

18. Go through stile in wall and again bear slightly right towards wall opposite

✓ **View of Robin Hood's Stride (rock formation) in distance ahead.**

19. Climb over stile in wall and continue on (wall on right)

20. Shortly, cross stile by gateway in this right-hand wall. Then, with your back to gateway, head diagonally left towards wall opposite and small wood

21. On meeting wall, cross stile, turn *left* and walk down (wall now on left)

22. On meeting wood, go through stile by gateway on left and then straight ahead (farm in distance on right)

23. Cross stile in wall and go straight on (path gradually becomes farm track)

24. Go through narrow stile by gateway and almost immediately follow wide track as it bears slightly left and *up*, round hill (ignore path through gate on right)

25. At bottom of track, turn *right* by old stone stile (looks like 3 stone pillars)

26. Head down hill (Youlgrave village church tower ahead, lake and farm on right)

27. Pass through thin line of bushes and trees and continue to head down (in direction of Youlgrave village)

28. Go over stile, across stream, straight on up hill and across towards right-hand corner

29. Cross stile by gateway and head straight down (wall on right). Go through stile by next gateway and follow track as it bears right

30. Go through next stile by gateway and head down right-hand wall towards houses

31. Shortly before houses, go through stile on right, bear slightly left and walk across to stile in wall. Pass through this stile and turn *right* down road

32. Cross bridge, turn *left*, go through gate and follow path alongside **River Bradford**

33. Continue along riverside, and *eventually* go through stile by gateway

✓ **House advertising 'Teas with Hovis' up lane on right serves refreshments in summer.**

34. Cross stone bridge, turn *right* and continue walking alongside river

✓ **We often notice large numbers of fish and also dippers (brown and white birds that dip up and down) along this part of the river.**

35. *Eventually*, go through gate, past wide, arched stone bridge and continue on (do not cross bridge). Later, as track crosses river, continue up (ignore paths off)

✓ **Foundations and ruins of several buildings can be seen around here. These are the remains of an old corn mill.**

36. Shortly after farm buildings, follow lane up and back to village centre

Walk 11

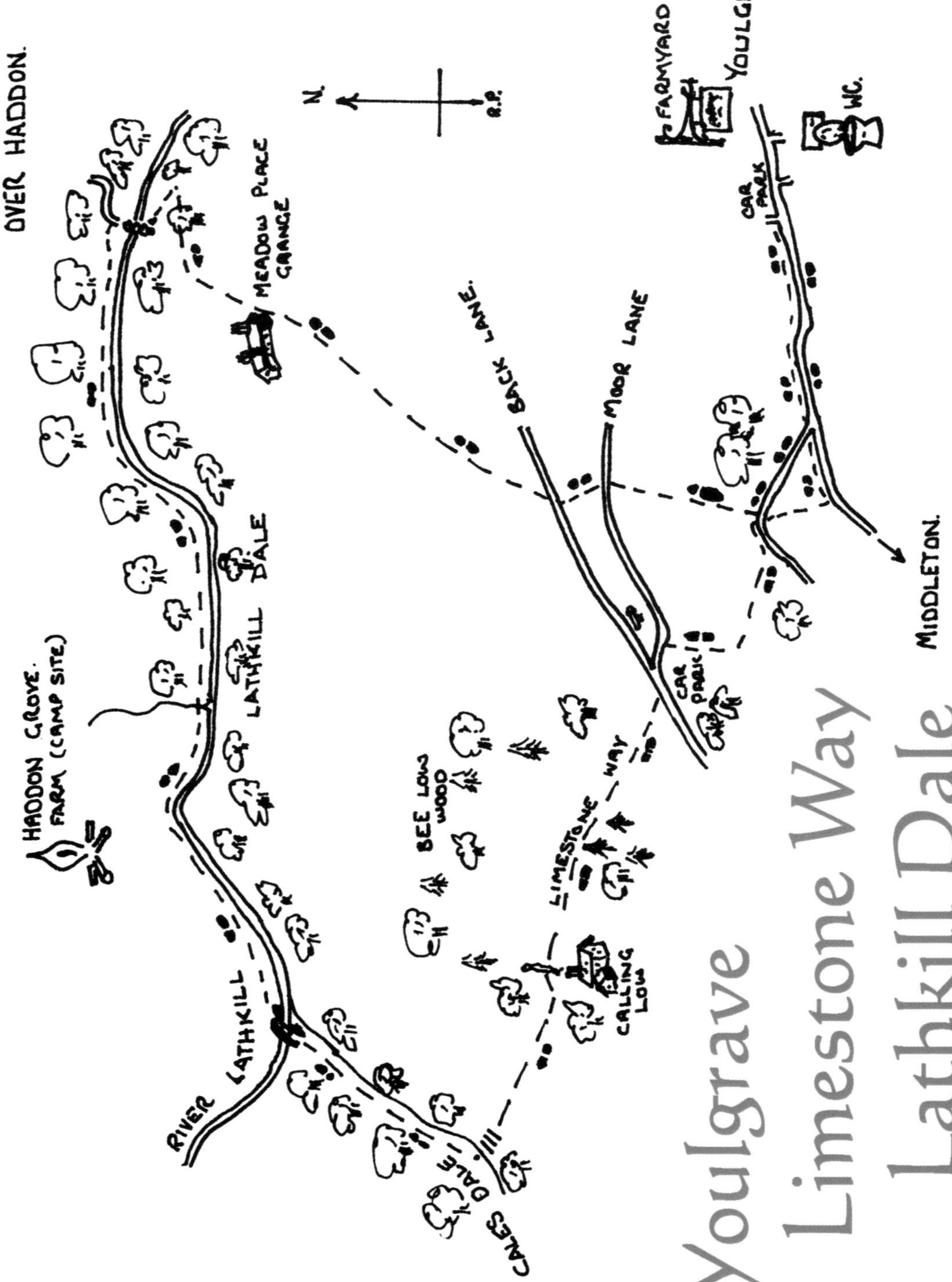

OVER HADDON.

MEADOW PLACE GRANGE

N R.P.

FARMYARD

YOULGREAVE

W.C.

BACK LANE.

MOOR LANE

CAR PARK

HADDON GROVE. FARM (CAMP SITE)

LATHKILL DALE

BEE LOW WOOD

LIMESTONE WAY

CAR PARK

MIDDLETON.

RIVER LATHKILL

CALLING LOW

CALES DALE

Youlgrave
Limestone Way
Lathkill Dale

Walk 11

Youlgrave - Limestone Way - Lathkill Dale

About this walk

This walk takes you along the popular Lathkill Dale with its steep rocky sides and rich variety of wild flowers. This National Nature Reserve boasts orchids, cowslips and the rare Jacob's Ladder. Lathkill Dale is a place of quiet beauty, but was once a scene of industry, based on a headlong rush for lead and, mistakenly, for gold - look out for Bateman's House, accessed by a small bridge.

Please note this route includes a concessionary path along part of the River Lathkill. The path is ***closed*** to the public on ***Wednesdays*** from ***October to January*** inclusive.

Distance	11km 6.7 miles
Terrain	A moderate walk with only short and gradual hills, near the start and towards the end. A lot of wide steps down to Lathkill Dale, and care needed as steps are uneven. A fairly long, easy stretch along the attractive dale. A mixture of footpaths, pavements, fields, steps, riverside and quiet lanes. Some areas can be muddy and uneven throughout the year.
Map	OS Explorer OL24 The Peak District, White Peak area. 1:25 000 scale.
Starting Point	Car park on the west side of Youlgrave (towards Middleton). This is off the main road running through Youlgrave, as houses finish (parking fee by donation). Public toilets in car park and village. Grid reference SK 205 640.
Refreshments	Youlgrave has a number of pubs and shops.

1. From car park, turn ***right*** up road. As road bends to right, carry straight on (sign posted **Middleton by Youlgrave**). Note that spelling is 'Youlgreave' on some maps.

2. As road bends to left, go through stile and small gate by large gateway on right and follow path up hill and slightly to the right

3. Go over stile in wall, cross road and turn ***left*** (ignore path ahead)

4. Follow road and just past bend, go over stile on ***right***. Bear left and head up hill to wall ahead

5. Go through gap in wall and follow path up hill (wall on left)

6. Near top of hill, bear right (away from wall) and continue up hill to top right-hand corner of field

7. Go over stile between 2 large gates (or through small gate behind large one)

8. Continue along path (wall on right). Path soon becomes track

9. As track meets lane (**Moor Lane**) by car park, turn ***left*** and walk along lane

10. On meeting road, cross this road, go through stile with small gate and take path heading diagonally across field

Bateman's House, Lathkill Dale

11. Go over stile in wall and head diagonally right to right hand wall. Then go over further stile with small gate

12. Continue along path as it heads diagonally left across field

13. At opposite side of field, cross stile and walk diagonally to right-hand corner. Go through gate and head along path (in **Low Moor Wood**)

14. Shortly go over stile in wall on right and head to corner of field by farm. Go through gate in wall just before farm entrance and head diagonally to gate in left-hand wall

15. Enter through gate and cross to right-hand corner of wood (farm on left)

16. Go through gate, across and through gate opposite

17. Cross next wooded area, go through gate and slightly diagonally right to further gate in right-hand wall close by

18. Continue to follow path to bottom right-hand corner of field. Go through gate and carry on as path bears right down hill

19. Go through further gate and continue diagonally down hill. Go through gate into Dale.

✓ **A mini gold rush hit this dale in 1854-56, after reports that gold had been found nearby. Overnight, people moved in to invest, but all was abandoned and much money lost, after it was found that there was little gold there.**

20. Go down wide slab steps (take care as these steps can be uneven) and at bottom cross stile and take path to right

21. Turn right as path joins another and then follow dale along

✓ **Lead has been mined over centuries in this area. One result of this was that the water table was lowered significantly, and in a drought the river can run almost dry - often in summer there is little more than a trickle here. The water drains to the 'soughs' (drainage tunnels which the miners dug).**

22. As path reaches river, cross bridge and turn *right* to walk alongside River Lathkill

23. *Eventually* path crosses stile into wood. (NB This is the start of a concessionary path that closes one day a week in winter - see 'About this Walk' page 71)

✓ **You will shortly see the columns of an old aqueduct, which once crossed the path taking water to the Mandale mine. The water was used to drive a large wheel which then pumped water out of the mine. This mine was worked from the 13th century until 1851, finally beaten by water problems.**

24. Continue along concessionary path

❖ **It is worth taking a look at Bateman's House and info boards, over arched wooden bridge. Then continue walk on original side of river.**

25. Eventually, on reaching houses, just after gate, turn *right* and cross footbridge

26. Turn *left* up track and follow track as it bends sharply to right

27. At top of track, go through gate and turn *left* towards farm

28. Go through farm's double gate and straight on through gateway just ahead. Then continue straight ahead, across farmyard, to stile in wall opposite, by gateways.

29. Go through further gateway and continue up (ignore path to Youlgrave going left up hill). Follow wall round to right

30. As wall bends to right, head diagonally left up field

31. Just over brow of hill, cross stile in wall ahead and bear slightly diagonally left to far left corner

32. Go over stile and slightly left up to stile near top left-hand corner. Cross this stile then cross road and go over stile opposite

33. Head straight down field to wall opposite, go over stile and follow path round to opposite wall

34. Cross stile then go straight across field to wall opposite

35. Go through stile by gateway, cross lane and through stile opposite

36. Go straight down field (wall on left) then through narrow stile and straight on (follow wall on left and pass a couple of derelict walls and gateways)

37. Go through further stile and head straight down towards road

38. Go through stile and gate, cross road, go over stile opposite and straight down

39. Go through gate and turn *left* along road to car park

Walk 12

Monyash
Lathkill Dale
Bagshaw Dale

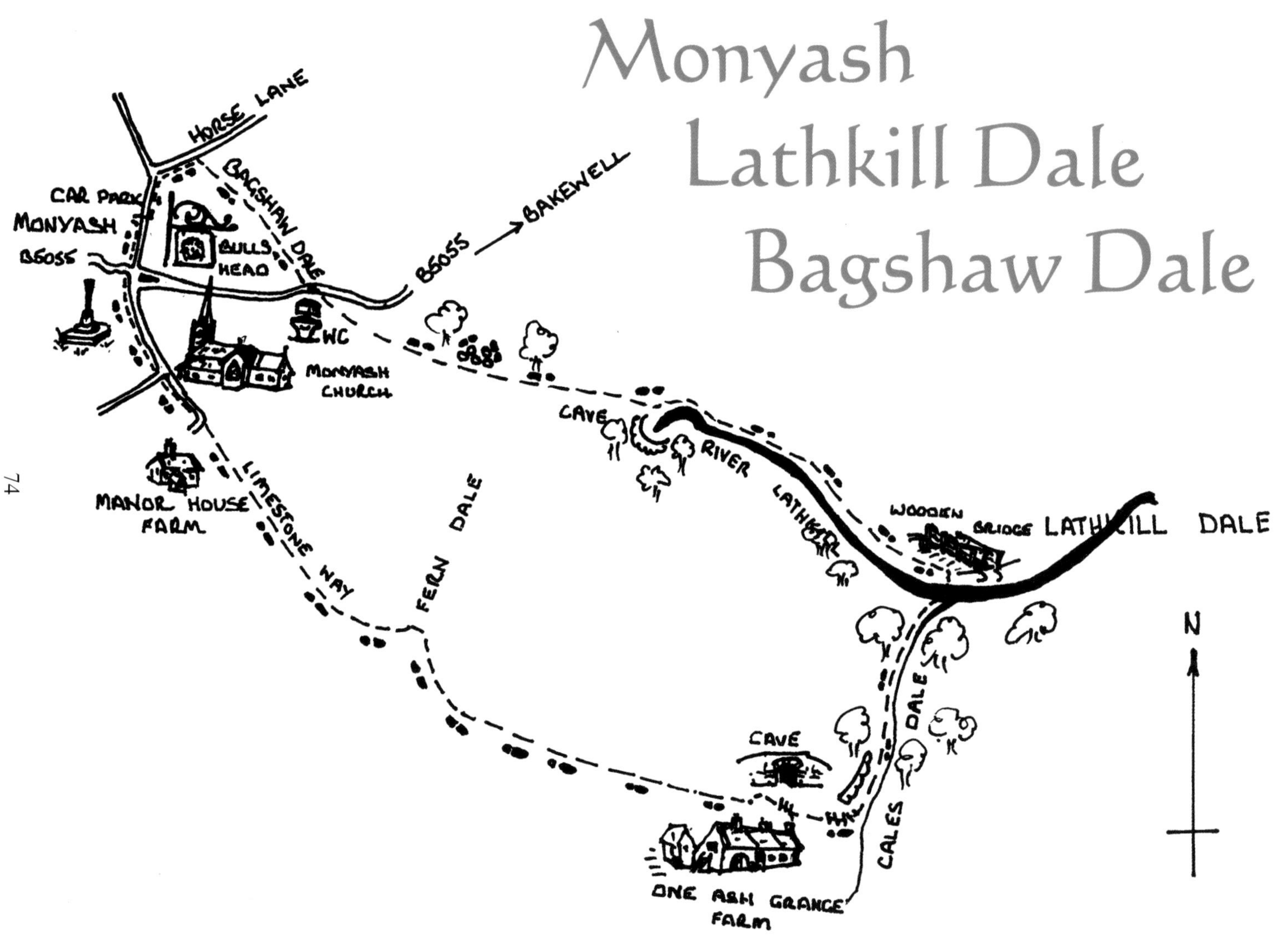

Walk 12

Monyash - Lathkill Dale - Bagshaw Dale

About this walk

The walk starts in the attractive village of Monyash, mentioned in the Domesday Book as Maneis, thought to mean 'many ash trees'. A really appealing combination of village, farmland and dales, with lovely views. Lathkill Dale is a place of quiet beauty, but was once a scene of industry, based on a headlong rush for lead and, mistakenly, for gold. A mini gold rush hit the dale in 1854-56, after reports that gold had been found nearby. Overnight, people moved in to invest, but everything was abandoned and a lot of money lost, after it was found that there was little gold to be had.

Distance	6.8km 4.2 miles
Terrain	This is not a demanding walk, with its mix of fields, paths, dales and rural lanes. Some care needs to be taken in a couple of places around One Ash Grange Farm, where there are rocky steps and a slightly tricky slope to negotiate. The attractive Lathkill and Bagshaw Dales have some very stony and uneven surfaces, especially around the old quarry area.
Map	OS Explorer OL24 The Peak District, White Peak area. 1:25 000 scale.
Starting Point	Car park (free) situated in Chapel Street, Monyash (off B5055). Grid reference SK 149 666. Public toilets towards end of walk.
Refreshments	Monyash has the Bulls Head Inn and a café open all year.

✓ **Before leaving car park, note information board on wall.**

1. From car park, turn *right* and walk up **Chapel Street**. Pass village green on left, cross road and head straight on (**Rakes Road**)

2. Ignore any paths to left or right. As road bends sharply to right, go straight on up lane (farm on right)

3. As lane bends right, carry straight on up track (**Limestone Way**)

4. Eventually, cross stile by gateway and continue (wall on right)

5. Very shortly, cross stile in wall on right and take path leading diagonally across field, to middle of far left wall

6. Go through stile and straight on (wall on left), then through gate and continue

7. Close to end of field, go over stile in wall on left and then turn *right*

8. Carry on down (keep wall on right) and at end of field go through gate on right and follow track towards farm (**One Ash Grange Farm**)

9. Just before entrance to private area of farm, turn *left* along track

✓ **This farm is one of the oldest in the area, having been founded in medieval times as an outpost of Roche Abbey in Yorkshire, a Cistercian order. The present farm buildings, though old, do not date so far back. Note also the ancient pig sties behind the farm and the cave on the left with arched entrance, probably used to store cheese.**

10. As track forks, take right-hand fork and go straight on to small wall between barns (do not turn right into farmyard)

11. Go through gap, down steep steps and straight on down path

12. Go through gate and continue down steep, rocky path

13. Near bottom of path turn *left* and follow path along dale

14. Cross bridge over **River Lathkill**, turn *left* and follow bottom path alongside river

Lathkill House Cave, which you will see shortly on your left, is the source of the River Lathkill. If the river is dry here, then it usually appears at some springs further down the valley. Centuries of lead mining in the dale have lowered the water table. This, combined with leakage of the river into nearby shafts, can reduce the river to a trickle, or to nothing, in summer.

15. Carry straight on along path and eventually go through kissing gate and straight ahead to wall opposite

16. Cross stile in wall by gateway and carry on

17. Go through further gate and then through final gate before road (toilets on left-hand side of road)

18. Cross over road and turn *left*. Very shortly turn *right*, go along path in front of buildings and over stile by gateway

19. Continue along track (through gateway) as it becomes a path (wall on left)

20. Go over stile in corner of wall and continue on to right-hand corner of field

21. Cross stile and carry on (wall on right). Pass through ruined gateway and go straight on

22. Continue through small gate in wall and carry on through 2 more stiles. Then turn *left* along road (**Horse Lane**)

23. At Junction, turn *left* to walk into **Monyash** and back to car park on right